The Golden Hour Dreamer

The Golden Hour Dreamer
Edited & Compiled by
Khushi Sharma

Paperback Edition

First published in India in 2023 by

Inkfeathers Publishing
Vivek Vihar, New Delhi 110095
www.inkfeathers.com

ISBN 978-93-90882-79-3

The Golden Hour Dreamer

Edited & Compiled by

Khushi Sharma

Inkfeathers Publishing
www.inkfeathers.com

Disclaimer

The anthology "The Golden Hour Dreamer" is a collection of 15 short stories and 6 poems written by 16 authors who belong to different parts of the world.

Unless otherwise indicated, all the names, characters, objects, businesses, places, events, incidents—whether physical/non-physical, real/unreal, tangible/ intangible in whatsoever description used in this book are either the product of the author's imagination or used in a fictitious manner. Any resemblance to actual persons, objects, entities, living or dead, or actual events is purely coincidental.

The contents published in this book are solely owned by their respective authors and are in no way intended to hurt anyone's religious, political, spiritual, brand, personal or fanatic beliefs and/or faith, whatsoever. In case, any sort of plagiarism is detected in the contents within this anthology or in case of any complaints, grievances, or objections, neither the anthology editor nor the publisher is to be held responsible.

I would like to dedicate this book to the most important person
I lost along the way. When I first started working on this anthology,
My Grandpa was my constant cheerleader; he must be an angel now,
blessing us all from above. Nanu, you are constantly missed,
I will always adore you, and I wish I could tell you sooner,
'We did it, Nanu!'

Curated with the writings of

Halo Golwin, Valerie Hernadez, Komal Joshi, Aanika G,

being_me_av, Debjyoti Das, Deborshmi Nath, Khushi Sharma,

Sandhita Agarwal, Mukul Namagiri, Ananya Purba,

Uma Bokil, Kai Jennings, Didriksha Chakraborty,

Arya, HyderK

Contents

Acknowledgements

I would like to thank everyone who has been my steady support system. I will never be able to thank my Mom and my Dad, I knew even if the world was against me, you always trusted me, and my entire family for believing in me. Cherry, my darling sister, you became my greatest hope and strength while working on this endeavour.

There are also some people who contributed to the creation of this anthology. My teacher of English language, Mr. S.C. Mahto who always encouraged me for pursuing language as my passion and career. He always said I possessed that spark. Mr. Paritosh Dubey, my mathematics teacher, who realized math was not my cup of tea and encouraged me to pursue language and offered me ideas for short tales and poems. There is also a person who does not want their identity to be revealed but they always comfort me with their words and stands like a pillar for me.

I am extremely grateful to Aastha and Mohisha Singh, my best friends for exposing me to literature and anime and for becoming my extended family at the last minute. Isaac Chen, another extended family for assisting me at the last minute with work, for always keeping an eye on me and for calming me down, as well as my friends Umang Lal and Akshay Kumar for always believing in me. Sneha Chowdhury, for being the older sister, mentor and support I always wished for. Thank you for providing me with so much affection.

I am grateful to all our Co-Authors for submitting their beautiful pieces for this anthology and for their patience throughout the entire process. Komal Joshi, you are so thoughtful; thank you for always checking on me.

I would like to express my heartfelt gratitude to the Inkfeathers family for including this naive editor among them, as well as Tanishk Singh (former Publishing Manager) for introducing me to this concept and paving the way for my hazy dreams to become a reality. Also, thank you to Uma Bokil (former Head of Publishing) for your unwavering support and for giving some great shape to my raw ideas. Sagar Kumar Bharadwaj (Founder and Director) for being very helpful in summarising the project in the end.

Your existence is a blessing to me! Thank you for having my back and trusting me.

Meet the Editor

Khushi Sharma is a young budding writer and an engineer-to-be from Ranchi who enjoys exploring and learning new things. She is a dreamer who does not believe in confining herself to who she already is. Since they touch on a variety of subjects, including nature, music, social issues, and more, her works are a reflection of who she is as a person. Writing stories came into the picture as a result of her lifelong love of reading and observing the world around her. She enjoys writing, painting and she is also a trained Kathak dancer.

Preface

It was back in 2021 when I thought of working for an anthology, to talk to new people, know about their dreams and fantasies and create a world which was different from the real world. As a child I was a fan of Harry Potter books and always wanted to live in a world like that. While growing up my best friend introduced me to Korean dramas and Animes. Eventually, it became my escape, an escape from my problems, toxic people and mainly the real world. I knew there were more people like me around the globe and hence this anthology was a road to connect with them. The whole journey of curating this anthology was fun and learning, every story submission I received, whether it was selected or not, was so full of dreams and fictional characters, and their passion. I deeply connected to all of them, cried, laughed, awed, and felt emotionally attached to each one of them. I was happy yet surprised that there were people who loved fiction. When I presented this theme to the Publishing Manager of Inkfeathers, he supported me with the idea and told me it was unique theme to work upon, and he was right, all the people I talked to, and their stories were unique. The title "The Golden Hour Dreamer" has its own story, I remember I pulled an all-nighter that day and I was in my room, reading and the clock strike 6.30 in the morning, the first sun rays came through my window, not very surprising I was dreaming while reading. I thought if there are daydreamers around the globe, may be all of them dreamed at this Golden hour and hence, it was named The Golden Hour Dreamer for the all the fellow daydreamers.

It gave me immense pleasure to work on something I always wished for. Who knew my escape would become my passion one day. The journey of curating this anthology was a bitter-sweet memory, most appreciated and some discouraged me of choosing a theme which was out of the box, but it was the passion of all the daydreamers or the golden hour dreamers who wanted the world to be seen through their eyes. I wanted to have stories which were all different from each other and had a new concept, I wanted this anthology to be confined yet impactful. I applied the Less is more concept to this anthology.

I think all of us daydreamers. We love stories; some real, some imaginary.

In this book, you will travel different worlds, worlds which are made my different astonishing writers, or I want to call them Daydreamers of every age group. So, dive into the world of dreams, fictional characters, aliens and may be ghosts!

I hope you connect with every story written by our extremely talented co-Authors.

Warm regards,

Khushi Sharma

Poetry

Before Tomorrow

by Uma Bokil

She tiptoed into the darkness one last time
and wore memories on her sleeves.
She soared with the ocean breeze
and dipped in the fragrance of the sea.

She bathed in starlight and sang to the moon.
She poured laughter into the lonely corners of gloom.
She drank and danced under a thousand shooting stars.
She poured honey nectar into the crevices of her scars.

She breathed in the sweetness of the air and filled her lungs to the brim.
Her wish for a fairyland had finally been fulfilled.
At least for a night, she was Universe's child,

Where she lived a life she deserved,
before tomorrow could arise.

Dreamer

by Itskomaljoshi

This word might be my favourite

Why you may ask well as a creative

I often dream vividly, spontaneously,
and sometimes a little too much

I am a dreamer, oh yes, I am

Dreaming at night or day dreaming, I can do both!

Sometimes it's doable and sometimes it's trouble
oh someone please break my thought bubble?!

Beautiful fairy-tale and crazy fantasies, that give us a sense of comfort and the will to explore and be more imaginative or could it be "dreams" as in "aspirations" or ambitions and the choice to choose more wisely, or do you mean those dreams which provide a refuge from the harsh reality such is life?

Either way it's good and a basic right to dream am I right?

My head is full of ideas crazy or bright?

That even I don't know ha-ha

I feel that I am judged at times muhaha

I read, 'for a life without dreams is barren and cold, like a bird with broken wings that cannot fly'

That hit me hard as that is such a sad image to paint so why not push and uplift yourself and those in need because you have two choices, the way I see it:

Flight or fight!

Win or to learn!

Conquer and celebrate life or to give in and accept defeat!

Simply up to you my friend so come on let's dream a little bit more shall we?!

Boulevard of Dream

by Khushi Sharma

The Journey towards the sunset boulevard,
She started to step forward.
It seemed like the way was easy and subtle,
But Life was full of obstacles
Empty mind and empty street,
She searched for the real side of her like a freak.
One body and Multiple roles,
Is this wanted the orthodox souls?

She was baffled,
She stepped towards her dream but stumbled.
She was pulled back,
Cause the society was full of dirty stack.

She wanted to express,
But kept behind the Veil.
She wanted to Fly,
But kept behind the cage.
And again, a dream was buried of a little sage.

The little feet refused to rest.
As she was not just a lamb but a tigress.
She turned the scratches into the batches.
They still tried to make her weak.
But now she already had the wings on fleak,
Who took off to fly high and free.
And stepped to her Boulevard of dream.

The Little Fly

by Sandhita Agarwal

The buzzy fly that wanted to go to the moon
To be the first fly there and become a national hero
First, he planned his sojourn in a tiny balloon
But soon he realized the error of his follies
He built a small red rocket for his trip
Equipped with all the things he would need
A tiny fridge with space snacks for months
A tiny suction toilet for his guts
The big day had finally arrived
He bade his goodbyes to his friends and family
His mother cried and cried for her crazy fly
But our hero was a determined guy
Away he went in his stuttering rocket
Dreaming of the moon's white surface
What if he meets some aliens there?

Then he will have so much to share
After a trip of 40 days, he did land
On the moon's white surface and empty sand
His rocket came crashing down
Without a noise, without a sound
Our little fly was in despair
He could breathe without air
The lunar surface did provide nourishment fair
But sadly, our little fly was forever stuck up there.

A Ladder to the Moon

by Didriksha Chakraborty

Brother, if only one day
I get a ladder this long,
That it can reach up to the moon and the stars
I will climb it with immense joy,
Even if I get tired
Or full of boredom

Will you accompany me then?
Let's climb together
Meet the tardigrades and rabbits staying there
Ask them to give us a boon
And we together will enjoy the serene view of the beautiful moon

The aliens staying there may find us peculiar,
Wondering from where we came
We may even get ambushed by them,
But you don't worry brother
I will befriend them with my witty tongue,
Encourage them to come to our delightful Earth
Give these humans down a frightful cheer

Don't you think by bringing aliens to Earth
Our fame will gear?

We will be known by people all around the world
The famous two who brought aliens to Earth
Why can't this happen true by chance?
I don't want to enjoy the beauty of the moon only while sitting in this Earth
I want to reach high up over that shiny ball
And enjoy its beauty from its topmost.

She Can Also Dream

by Ananya Purba Sengupta

They tossed their coins to guess the result,
And yes, the guess was right she was a girl.

Her first cry cheered everyone.
They started building their dream and expected it to be fulfilled by her,
But is this what she deserved?

As she entered the second phase of her life she was burdened with all the activities.

Everyone wanted her to be a perfectionist and forgot that,
she is too young to take the pressure of this gravity.
Crowded with the mountain of hopes and expectations,
they forgot to bring parity.

Girly should be her ambitions, restricted, should be her
dreams and be selected from the list provided by everyone.
But when she closed her eyes, she imagined beyond anyone.

The love for the soil, where she was born, the colorful
culture of her nation, the love for the people who gave her comfort,
made her feel she should give her return by putting in some effort.

Waking up to the chilly mornings, spending sleepless nights,
Celebrating all the festivals near the border with great pride.

Counting every breath of her life to be the last one,
Sharing her fate with her colleagues and getting honour
from the nation is what she wanted but there was no one
for her to guide.

Shedding blood for the nation, or fighting the enemies is not your job was being what taught to her,

All the paths that were selected for her will give her success in the future,

But dreams cannot be fulfilled through the eyes of others.

Everyone has the right to serve the nation

Girls can equally fight for the country and match their shoulders with equal passion. Open your eyes, spread your hand, and give her one chance

She will serve the nation and create history in her own fashion.

Stories

1

The Sleepless One

by Halo Golwin

So long as you believe you have escaped, you will remain imprisoned in the clutches of nightmares.

The genesis crux pierced through the cosmos of the Sketchbook Universe, creating the sentient soft toys, Teddy and Polar once again. The two soft toys woke up to the heavy beating of a father's heart.

'Sweet dreams will come true, my darlings......,' Teddy and Polar heard a deep and soothing voice.

Their creator was rocking them to sleep. Although they saw him as their only source of light, his eyes glowed with strange wistfulness.

'They look so happy, just like us,' Polar glanced over the cradles that carried the other soft toys.

It was strange how all of them bore a strange resemblance to Teddy and Polar.

'Goodnight Teddy...... Goodnight Polar' the father figure crooned, as they fell into a deep slumber.

In that moment, the Conscious drifted into oblivion, forcing the Unconscious awake.

A lush forest greeted Teddy and Polar. The landscape gleamed with velvet roses that glittered under the luminous stars. Giant burning glass shards carved out a peculiar symbol in the sky. A crimson moon towered above the forest, grinning mischievously at Teddy and Polar, while piano music seemed to drone on forever.

In a speck of pink mist, **the Sleepless One** emerged, his appearance concealed by a bubonic mask and a black coat.

'You all must be the latest versions to be recruited as truth-seekers......' the Sleepless One yawned.

The soft toys stared at the mysterious figure blankly. After a long pause, Polar finally spoke: *'What beckons us here?'*

'The nightmares are endless. Just crush them all for me...... Especially Your Worst Nightmare.'

'What's Your Worst Nightmare?' Polar enquired, as he fiddled with a velvet rose out of boredom.

'It takes on many forms and infiltrates into the deepest recesses of the mind. If the psychological defences are overwhelmed, you will be crushed,' the Sleepless One answered.

'What's crushed?' Polar was insistent on unravelling the truth.

'It's when a sentient being loses the will to live and becomes an empty vessel.' the Sleepless One replied lethargically.

Teddy and Polar grimaced at the notion of being crushed. Seems like in the Unconscious, it's crush or be crushed.

It wasn't long before the nightmares started harassing Teddy and Polar. At the chime of jingle bells, a giant Christmas bell appeared. Upon scrutiny, the duo found an intricate glass door and entered the bell.

'Aaahhh! A talking head! I was expecting gingerbread and cookies!' Teddy shrieked.

'My first customers! Just in time! I baked cookies for you all!' a decapitated head spoke earnestly.

'Let me try one!' Polar ate a cookie without hesitation, only to barf out a rainbow, along with a few mini unicorns that galloped away in annoyance. With a revolted look, Teddy politely rejected the cookies,

unknowingly invoking the talking head's fury.

'RING-A-DING-A-DING DONG!' the talking head slammed itself repeatedly against the bell, bleeding its head crimson.

'Aaahhh! My eardrums are going to burst!' Polar screamed.

'What? I can't hear you!' Teddy shouted in alarm over the ringing.

'Wait...... we don't have eardrums!' Polar reminded Teddy.

Upon Polar's sudden realization, the talking head transformed into a unicorn that galloped away happily ever after.

'You're a unicorn, Golwin!' a voice from the Conscious spilled into the Unconscious, filling the forest with a gentle light. Golwin must be the name of their father then.

It wasn't long before the nightmares lurking in the shadows struck again. From a dizzying bed of velvet roses, a defenceless toddler and a fair-skinned lady abruptly appeared.

'Read the Abstract for me!' the lady demanded the toddler, revealing a mountain of academic papers.

The toddler spoke eloquently: *'The emerging paradigm of lucid dreaming devices are reshaping the frontiers of night terror control and enabling new functionalities......'*

Despite the horrific volume of scientific jargon spoken by the toddler, the lady didn't budge.

'You're not reading me at all! I am not that Abstract!' the lady screamed and kicked the toddler repeatedly. Pools of crimson liquid oozed out of the disfigured body as it flailed its arms like a dead insect. Teddy and Polar recoiled in horror.

As the situation turned bleak, the Sleepless One appeared in a puff of pink mist and approached the lady unflinchingly. Upon unveiling his mask, the lady saw something worse than death. Try as she might, she couldn't escape his clutches. He slit both the lady and toddler's throats in an instant, putting them to sleep under a bed of crimson roses.

'Some nightmares cannot be salvaged. Crushing them is the only way,' the Sleepless One comforted Teddy and Polar whose living daylights had not yet returned to their faces.

'What's behind...... your mask?' Polar enquired meekly.

The Sleepless One flinched at the question before he disappeared.

White nights went by as Teddy and Polar were ruthlessly exposed to more horrors. While Teddy and Polar crushed most nightmares, they struggled to put some to sleep. In difficult times, the Sleepless One had to intervene.

'I'm getting sick and tired of this!' Polar whimpered as he hugged Teddy tightly. Teddy didn't have any comforting answers, so he found a velvet rose nearby and placed it on Polar's furry paws. Polar lightened up.

Despite getting increasingly lethargic from conquering nightmares every white night, Teddy remained optimistic. Perhaps the psychological defences of the Unconscious were steadily fortifying.

'So many of these velvet roses struggle to live on and blossom despite the minimal water and sunlight they receive. They're all symbols of hope, telling us not to give up!' Teddy encouraged.

'You're right, Teddy!' Polar exclaimed gleefully.

The cheerful atmosphere didn't last long as the Sleepless One appeared once more, interrupting the heartfelt moment.

'It seems like the time has come again. The nightmares will never end,' the Sleepless One yawned.

'Stop back-facing us! I need to confirm something,' Polar sounded

unusually cranky from his lack of sleep. Before Teddy could swipe the mask off the Sleepless One, he vanished in a cloud of pink mist, causing him to inhale some drowsy chemicals.

Teddy and Polar knew they couldn't fall asleep as the nightmares will continue to run rampant.

On another white night, Teddy and Polar saw the Sleepless One collapse on the ground, after putting more nightmares to sleep. They rushed to give first aid to him, conveniently forgetting that they were just imaginary soft toys created from the stardust of the Sketchbook Universe.

'Don't get too close to me...... I don't want anyone to see me in my darkest hour......' the Sleepless One cried out.

Teddy and Polar simply ignored his dying wishes. It was then that the light from the crimson moon carelessly spilled onto the mask of the Sleepless One. Cracks momentarily formed on the mask, unveiling a part of his face.

"No......!" the Sleepless One cried out again.

Teddy caught a glimpse of his face and was rendered speechless.

'I can't believe...' Before Teddy could complete his sentence, the Sleepless One smacked Teddy unconscious and fled.

'Wake up! Wake up......!' Polar nudged Teddy, checking for any signs of the Conscious in the Unconscious. At least Teddy's heart was still beating steadily.

Teddy woke up in a jolt and shrieked: *'Aahhhh! A nightmare!'*

'No Teddy, it's just me, Polar. Tell me what you saw!' Polar implored.

'He...... I think he might be our father, and the reason we are born into this world,' Teddy blurted out in disbelief.

Polar was getting pessimistic, but he was persistent in finding out more.

'Why does he hate nightmares so much? Can't he crush them by himself?' Polar deliberated.

Teddy had a sudden epiphany: *'Maybe the Sleepless One is Your Worst Nightmare, since even the nightmares are terrified of him.'*

As Teddy and Polar were still stumped, the next wave of nightmares was fast approaching.

In the distance, Teddy and Polar saw a little boy. They inched closer to investigate.

'I'm going to become multifaceted, just like a flawless diamond!' the boy grinned cheerfully as he stabbed himself repeatedly with thin glass.

Against the backdrop of velvet roses, Teddy, and Polar saw crimson again. As the boy was about to stab his own eye, Teddy intercepted the boy's hand with his signature Taekwondo technique, while Polar karate-chopped him to the ground.

'Stop trying to be perfect, boy!' the Sleepless One appeared and revealed his face once more.

This time, the nightmares did not seem to fear his face as much as before. The boy only yawned before reluctantly falling asleep.

'My control is weakening...... The tragedy is going to repeat again......'

Unexpectedly, the Sleepless One took down his mask, revealing his face to Teddy and Polar.

'I knew it! You're our father after all! We're so happy to see you!' Teddy beamed with joy.

The Sleepless One appeared crestfallen, but Teddy and Polar couldn't understand why.

Tears welled up in the eyes of the Sleepless One as he spoke: *'You all exceeded my expectations in crushing nightmares. I'm proud of you all. I promise I would give you all sweet dreams for all of eternity......'*

Soon, the pink mist emanating from the Sleepless One developed into a menacing storm.

The drowsiness was in full force now.

'Goodnight Teddy...... Goodnight Polar......' the Sleepless One crooned. He carried the two soft toys in his arms as they fell into a deep lull under a bed of crimson roses.

'Stop tickling me, Polar......' Teddy muttered.

'Heehee, unicorns......' Polar mumbled.

So long as you believe that sleep is an escape, you will never unravel the truth behind the darkest nightmares.

Teddy and Polar were crushed once again. The crimson moon snickered mischievously again, but The Sleepless One simply giggled back at it.

He chuckled obnoxiously: *'Time to create more versions of them! Soon, their dream magic shall grow strong enough with stardust to crush me. Then, I no longer have to mourn their deaths!'* The Sleepless

One shielded Teddy and Polar against the tempest of crimson knifes that desecrated the earth predictably every time they were crushed. The knifes only tickled him as they seared into his flesh.

The velvet roses were always a symbol of hope, but underneath them lies the unspoken tragedy of broken dreams. The typhoon of pink mist emanating from the Sleepless One blew away all the velvet roses, revealing countless corpses of Teddies and Polars.

'Please! Anything but CRIMSON! That DISGUSTING, FILTHY and WRENCHED colour!' Golwin woke up in a startle. He was awake again. He gaped in horror as his worst fears were realized. Finally, the moon had bled crimson in the Conscious world.

Golwin contemplated: Cursed with eternal insomnia and his unquenchable pink mist, the Sleepless One could only repent by putting the nightmares he conjured to sleep. All Teddies and Polars created from the Sketchbook Universe had failed to crush him, for which he so desperately wished.

Still, how could he bear to see them get crushed repeatedly even if their deaths aren't real?

Startled from his nightmare, Golwin held onto Teddy and Polar dearly, only to catch a strange blue tint in their bead-like eyes. He couldn't believe it.

People say that the eyes are windows to the soul, but since Teddy and Polar didn't have souls, they only reflected what he desperately wished to see in himself.

Mimicking the Sleepless One, Golwin chuckled obnoxiously: *'I will fulfil my promise! Teddy and Polar will be having sweet dreams soon!'*

In a rush, he collapsed all his remaining hopes and dreams into a supernova, pouring all the stardust he could muster into drawing his final version of Teddy and Polar in the Sketchbook Universe.

I will crush the Sleepless One by myself! This time, I won't let Teddy and Polar be crushed!

Once in a blue moon, a miracle might save him from the Sleepless One. Golwin believed he saw the reflection of the moon in their eyes, but the moon wasn't blue, and he had already crushed himself.

2

Whispers of the Demon

by Deborshmi Nath

There once was a boy called Sam who lived in Holland with his Aunt Sally and Uncle Bern in a small house. Sam was already 12 years old, studying in a public school nearby. He had a 7-year-old sister called Ginny and an 8-year-old brother called Billy. One day, Uncle Bern brought them each a small glittering ball and handed them to the kids after work. When they each got it, they wanted to wash their balls since they were a bit dusty and washing them could make them clearer. But as soon as they finished wiping their balls and lifted their heads back up, they were astonished to find a totally different place standing in front of their eyes. Instead of the bathroom sink in front of them or Uncle Bern and Aunt Sally's room on their right, they saw a small river swiftly flowing in front of their eyes and woods on their two sides from which birds sang loudly at the water's sight. They crossed the river easily since there was already a line of rocks through the river as if awaiting them. Suddenly a small squirrel came squeaking over and pulled Ginny's dress with his teeth towards the woods. It was almost impossible to get rid of it, and so they had to follow him. Astonishingly, the squirrel released Ginny and took them to a boy about the same age as Sam himself. The boy had brown hair, blue eyes like marbles, and red freckles. He was riding a fair brown horse, and he had a bow in his hands with an arrow ready on string.

He started to speak to them as soon as he laid his eyes on them,

'Hello newcomers, I am Prince Ryan and my father, King Hildron, is the King of Bilima. May I please know your names?'

'Hi Prince Ryan, I am Billy, this is my brother Sam, and this is my sister Ginny.' introduced Billy as he pointed to Sam and Ginny,

'We have come from Holland by this mysterious ball that our uncle gave to us.'

'Do you mean that the three of you have come from another world? We do not recognize any place known as Holland.' Said Prince Ryan.

'Well, we do not know any place called Bilima either.' Replied Sam.

'We haven't had any dinner yet, may we get some food, Prince Ryan?' asked Ginny for the first time. At that moment, nobody knew why but Prince Ryan started to laugh so hard that later he even complained about having a stomach ache.

'Yes, sure Ginny, just come and follow me' answered Prince Ryan still in his laughing situation. He got off his horse and guided them to a palace. The palace from the outside was mostly white with the roofs all red. They went in and met a man who at once they knew was King Hildron because of his royal throne and the golden crown that stood upon his head.

'May I welcome all of you to my palace; I am King Hildron and am the 11th king of Bilima. I am sure you have already met my son, Prince Ryan. Our kitchen will serve food for us in a minute so Prince Ryan will lead all of you to your own rooms that we have chosen for our guests and their you boys and girls can get some clothes that one of our staffs will serve to you. Please come back to eat after you are done, and I will meet you kids right there.' Said King Hildron as he welcomed them. They walked upstairs with Prince Ryan quietly and then he showed each of them their rooms. He also introduced them to a kind lady staff, Ms. Honey. They got new pairs of clothes that she gave them and walked back downstairs when they saw King Hildron smiling and

waiting for them besides a table full of food. They sat around the table ready to pick up their forks. They had turkey, chicken curry, both fried and boiled fish, fried rice, salad, Bilimain ice cream and a huge Bilimain jam-tart. They enjoyed the food. *'Thank you so much!'* exclaimed Sam. *'May I get some water?'* Sam asked when suddenly Prince Ryan's expression changed. His smile faded away; his eyebrows lowered, and his eyes became smaller.

'What's wrong Prince Ryan?' asked Billy, *'Why do you look so upset?'* The three of them looked really confused, but the room kept silent for a moment but was disturbed by King Hildron's sigh.

'It is a big problem that our Bilima is right now facing so we need help. It is said that up in those snowy western mountains, there lives a giant creature that has closed a lot of the resources from where us Bilimains used to get water, because of him we now only have a few available places to get water from.' explained Prince Ryan slowly.

'Oh, just think about how bad it is to one day run into such a problem!' said Ginny.

'Okay, but it is not the time to think about all of that, what if we help? I think we might be able to help these Bilimains with this problem if we go for it.' announced Sam. Prince Ryan's eyes widened and brightened; he couldn't speak but by his face they knew he wanted to say something.

'But you are only kids and are our guests, how can you three be sent to go in for such a danger?' said King Hildron.

'Don't worry, we will be just fine. It isn't a matter to risk three kids for one big country.' urged Billy.

'Ok fine.' sighed King Hildron, *'but none of our soldiers can be able to help you because our Royal Sorcerer had once found out that no Bilimain can ever destroy that monster, so that means only outsiders like you children can do something to help. How about starting your journey tomorrow before sunrise, then? Food will be packed ready for all of you*

tonight, if you are finished, you children can head back to your rooms.'

They all went back upstairs and rushed back to their own rooms after saying Goodnight. Ms. Honey took great care of all of them and spent her night with Ginny since the room that Ginny got had a bunk bed. The next morning, Ms. Honey gave them good warm clothes for their journey and after they got nice and ready, they saw Prince Ryan and King Hildron sitting royally in the main court with their beautiful crowns on their heads. The three of them gave a nice bow in the style that we do in our own world, but Prince Ryan and King Hildron gave back their bows in their own Bilimain way.

'Good morning, friends, how was last night's rest?' asked Prince Ryan.

'Awesome!' replied Billy.

'Please follow Prince Ryan to the stable to get your favorite or the strongest horses and I shall meet you back there by the gate.' said King Hildron. Prince Ryan stood up and took them to the Royal Stable. Ginny Ginny wanted a mare, so Price Ryan recommended her a gorgeous and gentle mare called Snowflake. It was hard for Sam and Billy to choose one because the stable was huge, and it was full of horses they appreciated. Some sniffed at them and neighed, while others neighed at the basket of carrots nearby, and the boys fed the horses. There were two horses that appreciated the two boys' feeding and care so much that they stuck their heads out of the stable, eager to let the boys have a ride on them. Elliot and Sharp-Eye were led out of the stables along with Snowflake. Snowflake was a perfectly white and beautiful like a snowflake with white mane and dark brown eyes. It seemed to be that Snowflake and Ginny admired each other very much, but Sam had to help Ginny up because Snowflake was a tall, long-legged horse. Elliot and Sharp Eye were both twins, so they looked pretty much alike. They were both light brown horses with dark brown mane and had a stripe of white mane across the middle of their foreheads; these two horses were very fast and strong. *'I am so*

sorry that I couldn't go with you three because father just doesn't allow me to go into such a danger.' said Prince Ryan, *'But stay safe and I am sure you three will do it. Oh, and I totally forgot to give this to you last night friends, one of our soldiers found this on that mountain a few months ago. This sheet of paper has three riddles and if you solve them, you probably will get some help or clue.'*

'Don't worry, we shall try our best!' replied Sam. The three waved at Prince Ryan and King Hildron but in a moment, they were ready to set out with the horses. They didn't have any problems with the horses since they all had horse riding classes after school back in Holland three times a week. After sunrise the sunlight was roasting their faces with all that heat and light and so they decided to start reading the sheet of paper that Prince Ryan gave to them. It was rolled tidily inside Sam's pocket. So, Sam started to read it out loud while Billy and Ginny listened. *'Looks like there is enough light now, so I am going to read the sheet of paper with the riddles that Prince Ryan gave me out loud. One, I am a place where some wild animals live in, sometimes people come inside me to investigate, and in old times, people would make a type of art on my inside. Two, I am closed but you can always open me. I am used for putting things inside me and some of my kind even have a hole where people can poke a stick to open me. When I am opened, I get split into two but beware of what is inside me. Three, I am blue and is hung on a string. I am very expensive if you buy me, and I never come off or stick but I get done by a knot. I die, the water begins.'*

'How should we ever be able solve these clues? They sound pretty hard; gosh somebody could help us.' exclaimed Ginny as she sighed. They started to think for a few minutes when their silence was broken by a voice they couldn't recognize. They raised their heads and saw an old man staring at them. He had a long white beard which hung down his cheeks and made him look very wise. He had long eyebrows and blue eyes that glittered in the daylight. He was wearing a blue and golden traditional Bilimain clothes and had hair growing down to his

neck. *'Hello, I am Ginny, these are my brothers Sam and Billy.'* introduced Ginny as she pointed at them.

'Hi kids, I live in another village besides Bilima alone in a small cottage and my name is Mr. Gilbert. I come to these grasslands every day because of how quiet it is for an old man like me to rest and calm in peace.' said the old man. Then, Sam told him everything about where they were going and why. *'I know all about it, I am the Royal Sorcerer of Bilima. If you wish, I can give you some things that may help you.'*

'Thank you so much Mr. Gilbert.' laughed Ginny. The old Mr. Gilbert put one of his hands on top of the other and closed his eyes. The next moment he separated his hands again and there was an arrow and a quiver between his hands. He handed them to Sam and did the same thing again twice. But the second time he gave Ginny a compass and the third, gave Billy a ball around the same size as the ball that Uncle Bern had given him. *'These aren't normal ones, Sam, if you use this bow, you can always shoot an arrow straight into the very place that you want to shoot it to. Ginny, if you use this compass, you can be able to go anywhere you want if you tell the compass where and follow it. Billy, if you look carefully into this ball, you can always know what now what is happening in any place you want to see. Good luck kids, stay safe, but I cannot give away the fact whether you should succeed or fail, but what I can tell you is always have hope in yourself.'*

'Wow!' exclaimed Billy.

After that, he had left and Sam had checked his watch, they realized that it was long past lunchtime and how hungry they were. As the old man had said that they were in a large grassland, they got off their horses and took off their saddles before the horses bent down for grass. The palace's kitchen had packed them a lot of Bilimain chicken sandwiches of which they only ate some from each of their baskets and took some rest on the soft relaxing grass. But their journey soon began once again. Ginny got onto Snowflake by herself this time because Snowflake bent down and cooperated as well. Snowflake felt very nice when Ginny kept on playing with her soft mane as they went on trotting on the grass. They were just going to cross a little creek that was crinkling in front of their eyes when they saw that the sun was setting. They went on for another hour when they decided to spend their night under a large and thick tree that was on their left. The got off and took off their saddles from the horses before settling down for their rest. Sam and Billy lied on the opposite side of Elliot and Sharp Eye, but Ginny lied right beside Snowflake's legs. Ginny and Billy fell asleep as soon as they rested their heads on the grass, but Sam stared at the beautiful night sky for a while before he had closed his eyes as well. The next morning, Billy was the first one to wake up and he called Sam and Ginny up and then they had some delicious fruits from neighboring trees, but the sweetest ones were on the Jackal berries. The three found their muscles to be as stiff as ever and hard to move around, but they managed it. They went back onto the horses in a while and they were on the track again, by lunchtime they were already a bit uphill and then the horses suddenly stopped in front of a dark cave, when an idea suddenly popped into Sam's mind. *'Ginny, Billy, don't you two think that the first riddle can be a cave?'* said Sam but the other two looked kind of confused so he went on, *'see, caves are home to different animals and some scientists come to investigate caves, ancient people that lived on Earth a long time ago used to make cave paintings on the sides of the caves with different colored rocks.'*

'Then what are we waiting for? Let's go in!' exclaimed Ginny as they got off the horses.

'Wait but, how do we know if it is this cave or not?' asked Sam, *'Well, I guess all we can do is to go in and check it out.'* Sam and Billy were together in front of Ginny since they were earlier to get off the horse and come inside the cave, but this order changed in a moment when Ginny suddenly rushed in between Sam and Billy to stop them from moving on and exclaimed, *'The second riddle must be a box then! That's because a box is closed but you can always open it and you use a box for*

putting things inside. Some boxes have key holes for keys to get put in, and half of the box is the lid, so the box gets split into two parts just like the sheet of paper had said.' exclaimed Ginny as she rushed through her evidence.

'There's our sister's brain!' said Billy the next moment as Sam gave Ginny a nice, good high-five.

'But don't you two think that it's too dark in here? I think we better go back out to light some fire with us so that we can see better in this dark cave.' suggested Sam. So, they all ran back out from the cave and looked for some sticks or branches on the floor. They had completed it in a while, so they went in again with a stick in their hands that had fire caught to its top. They walked for a long time but stopped when they found out that they had already walked from the mouth of this cave until its very end. *'What? Does this mean that we must get back out of here and start that riding again until we find another cave now?'* groaned Billy unhappy and tiredly.

Read the next section to find out what happens...

3

The Twilight Heroes

by Deborshmi Nath

Ginny, Billy, and Sam had come to the wrong and innocent cave. They had to walk back out again into the warm morning sunlight and had to start their journey again. Suddenly, Ginny's eyes widened, *'Oh, why didn't I think of this before? What if we use the compass that Mr. Gilbert had given me?'*

So, Ginny took it out of her pocket and spoke out, '*the correct cave we are looking for.*' Then started leading in the front. They went on for another three days with their same routine before meeting another cave. This time, they were at a lot higher altitude up on the mountains and it seemed like the cave was even darker the last one, especially because it was almost time for sunset. So, they had to light fire onto some sticks just as they did the last time. After a few more minutes of walking, a bright blue box came into their sight. The box looked perfectly carved with golden edges and dark blue patterns. Billy was just about to open the box when Sam remembered the last part of the second riddle. It had said to beware of the thing inside, so he shouted, 'Wait!' and so Billy dropped the box right out of his hands immediately. The box gave a loud *thump* s it hit the floor. Sam said, *'We must be prepared to run for our lives as soon as I give you the orders, there might be something dangerous inside. Do you understand me?'* And the two nodded at him. Slowly they opened the box and Ginny was already facing the other way shutting her eyes with her hands, she was terribly afraid. It was a very scary, big monster that came out of the box. The monster matched with what the box looked like, but the monster, unlike the box, looked very ugly. He had big dark spots and green smaller spots all around his body. He also had a huge snot hanging down his nose and, most terrifyingly, his feet faced one to the front and the other to the back. The monster had two big horns on his head, six long arms and a big fat belly even compared to his height. He bent down to see their faces which looked like ants to him and was just going to pick Ginny and Billy up when Sam had screamed, *'Run!'* For a long time, they did not even know or realize what they were doing but their legs went on faster than ever. Their speed was so unbelievable that if you had watched this moment in front of your eyes, you may have thought that these kids could have broken our world's record.

When they had finally reached the mouth of the cave, in their minds they felt like it took them forever to run back out. They were all panting so hard that the moment they had stopped their legs, they dropped off to more of a lying position than a sitting one.

'Ho-w man-y ba-ll-oo-ns do-es he ha-ve in hi-s hu-ge bel-ly?' asked Ginny, stopping for her breathe every moment. *'It looked like at least six times of you. But okay, we can still do it if we try our best. While we take a rest, shouldn't we think about the answer to the last riddle? I am pretty sure that if we solve it, we will know what to do next.'* said Sam, still needing some breathe sometimes as well. Then he took out for once again the sheet of paper that Prince Ryan had given them. They all thought for a long time about it very quietly when Sam spoke again, *'Might it be a bag or a purse?' 'I didn't see any bags or purses with the monster or around it.'* replied Ginny. *'But can it still be a bottle, a mug, or a jug since those things can hold water in it?'* But this time Billy shook his head which seemed to mean that her guess maybe wasn't that right. By this time, they were all calm and normal again except Ginny. She

had to keep up with the two fast brothers in order not to get apart from them.

But Billy thought about something else in his mind, *'Don't you think it can be the gem that the monster was wearing as a locket on his neck? Because as I remember that gem was almost bumping into the back of my head, it was blue and he had it hung on his neck by a string, so he must have done a knot to the string to tie it up. Then after he ties it, the gem will neither stick to his body, nor will it come off. If you go to a store, gems like that one must cost a lot.'* Billy described.

'Yippee!' exclaimed Ginny *'Were coming monster, start getting ready to get defeated! But Billy, do you mean that we somehow need to break the gem as the last line in the riddle says?'* asked Ginny.

'Yup, I guess that's the thing we've got to do.' answered Sam.

'But how are we supposed to do that?' asked Ginny again curiously.

Back in the dark cave the monster stood there until the kids were out of sight. Then he started to speak to himself, *'These Bilimains think they can just come and spoil my plan. Do they even know who I am and what I can do? Let them come, let them come, they don't even know what to do, they think they can get their water back just by killing me. This time they seem to have sent these three tiny babies to kill me, I am starting to feel too bad for that King Hildron.'* muttered the monster and by the time he had finished, he started to laugh as loud as ever. He decided to go back into the box if anyone else comes over again.

You are probably thinking about how such a giant monster like him could ever fit in such a box because even if us humans try to fit inside, only about half of our body might fit inside. But the monster has made himself a potion that can turn him to a size as small as a new born baby and he has made the potion so that whenever he comes out, he will return to his own and normal size again. The three brothers and sisters had made their plans for what they are each going to do after they go inside. So, they tiptoed back in the cave and after a while of walking, they saw the same blue box that they had opened earlier. It had the same blue patterns and the same golden edges, but somehow it gave them a different spirit just by looking at it now. Following the first part of their plan, they all burnt off their fires before opening the box so that the monster this time could not see so clearly and the box was lonelily placed by the wall on the right side of the cave just like it had been the last time, they had seen it. They slowly opened the box again, and the same thing began to happen, though they couldn't see his appearance so well this time. He came out again and roared, *'Who is this devil that opened my box again? You three insects of King Hildron's again?'* None of them replied but kept quiet. Still not making a noise, Ginny and Billy sneaked to the back of him and started to climb up his huge leg while Sam was taking out his bow and his quiver that was full of arrows. Ginny and Billy were climbing up the monster's body while tickling him with their hands. It may sound like an easy job for the two of them, just as they had imagined earlier, but it was a lot harder when they began doing it. The monster could speak just like us, but he was wild; so, he neither had a bath in his life, nor did he ever cook his food before eating. But the two of them had to journey through most of his body; from his feet, to his elbows, and up to his neck. So, think about how that would feel if you had to do that same thing, I probably would have fainted in the end.

Finally, Sam had done his aiming and just as Mr. Gilbert had said, his arrow shot right into the middle on the beautiful blue gem that the monster was wearing. It fell to the floor crashing with a sound like glass and broke into a million pieces. When Ginny and Billy realized what had just happened, they slid straight down to the bottom of his legs and came rushing towards Sam. Ginny slowly picked up one tiny broken piece but by the time she opened her hand, it had disappeared within thin air. Slowly the monster also faded away with the pieces. *'Yes!'* exclaimed Ginny, *'We have defeated that blue, ugly, huge, spotted creature! And plus, how could anyone, even if it's a twenty-five feet tall monster, defeat such awesome rangers like us?'*

'Yes, Ginny we did it and are the two of you alright after visiting through his lovely body?'

All of a sudden, a young lady came to them out of nowhere and said, *'Hello friends nice to meet you all, thank you so much for saving me from the monster, Kentile. I am the guardian of all the water sources in Bilima and my name is Mirana, but Kentile had locked me up into that gem.'*

Sam asked curiously, *'But why did he do that to you?'*

'He wanted to rule over Bilima,' she explained. *'The first dragon of Bilima was the water dragon, he had chosen me to be the guardian. He had said that as soon as I am away from water, most of the water sources in Bilima will dry out. So Kentile had somehow found out about me and planned to stop all of Bilima's water and then challenge King Hildron.'*

'Oooh, I see' said Ginny nodding her head.

'Umm friends, I think it's time for me to go back down underwater. All our Bilimain friends are probably waiting for me. Bye!'

That was her last word when she disappeared with the air, before the three could ask any more.

'I'm starving after all of this.' groaned Ginny, *'I can eat a horse like a piece of cake right now!'* So, they all enjoyed rest of the sandwiches that were left in their saddles and then started galloping back towards King Hildron's palace with Snowflake, Elliot, and Sharp Eye. It didn't take long before they reached the day after the next; they got in the palace before sunrise and had some rest back in the rooms. Their breakfast was ready in an hour and Ms. Honey called them all downstairs as soon as one of the kitchen maids informed her. King Hildron, Prince Ryan and the three children all sat around the breakfast table and served themselves with the eggs, sandwiches, sausages, breads, muffins, juices, and mugs of water. *'For the riddles, Prince Ryan, Sam got the answer to the first one was a cave, and it was where the monster lived. Oh yeah, I almost forgot to tell you that his*

name was called Kentile. Then the answer to the second one, which was the one that I came up with, was a box. Finally, our smart brother Billy got the answer to the last riddle, and it was a piece of gem that the monster had hanging on his neck like a locket...' explained Ginny through most of the meal. She slowly told their whole story to King Hildron and Prince Ryan who seemed like, to Billy and Sam, that both were into the story with Ginny while she explained. Ginny always had an own ordered way of telling her stories, so the listeners would never find it tedious. But something suddenly rang into Sam's mind. *'How are we supposed to go back to Holland now?'* asked Sam very seriously. Ginny was still telling her story until Prince Ryan and King Hildron realized what was going on and their faces changed.

'Wait, but before that, shouldn't we go and return the things that Mr. Gilbert had given us?'

'Oh yes, I totally forgot about that.' Ginny remembered, 'But how?' Before any of them could reply, Mr. Gilbert appeared right in front of their eyes smiling.

'Kids, I am so proud of how you three have saved Bilima. So, I would like you all to keep them, it might help you in the future again. Bye!'

'Bye' they all whispered after he was gone.

'Hmmm, now to go back home, don't you two feel like it might work if we try to wash our balls again?' suggested Billy. *'Well, we can try with that, probably!'* answered Ginny slowly and quietly. *'So, if we must test it, we'd better hurry up. Uncle Bern and Aunt Sally must be very worried about us.'* said Sam. Billy took out his present from Mr. Gilbert and looked into the ball to see what Aunt Sally and Uncle Bern were doing, they were also having breakfast, but the entire table was filled with Aunt Sally's tears while Uncle Bern tried to stop her. *'It has already been like a week since my kids were missing, and you expect me to calm down and have breakfast cheerfully?"* Billy lifted his head back off the ball and looked quite surprised at how time had gone by so fast. *'Yes, it's surely time to leave, they're all so worried about us!'*

They said goodbye to King Hildron and Prince Ryan and then rushed to the bathroom and turned on the roaring tap. One by one, they slid their hands and balls right under the water and, at once, were back into their old bathroom besides Ginny's bedroom, they were back at home. They walked out to check whether Aunt Sally or Uncle Bern was at home or not when they heard a squeak from somewhere and again it went. Ginny looked down and saw that it was the same squirrel that they had first met when they were just new to Bilima. It had been on Ginny's shoulder when she washed her ball. *'Where have the three of you been, my dear darlings? Your uncle and I were so worried about you that–huh, I can't really explain. We went asking as many people on the street as ever!' 'U-u-u-um, we went to my classmate, Claire's house for a sleepover.'* said Ginny managing to make up something for Aunt Sally. *'Okay kids, now I see.'* said Aunt Sally with a deep sigh. In a few days they had named their Bilimain squirrel as Gloria and she gave them all the happiness year after year. They saved their special glittering balls in a very safe and nice area so that they could always remember King Hildron, Prince Ryan, old Mr. Gilbert, Mirana, and their adventure in Bilima. Just those few days had changed life in a different World and the lives of three amazing rangers. Back in Bilima, year after year and generations after generations, they would pass on the story of the three children saving Bilima from that cruel devil who wanted to rule over Bilima and stole Mirana to block Bilima's water.

Years passed by in Holland as well, Ginny, Billy and Sam kept it a secret memory in their heart!

4

What Are Dreams Made of

by Valerie Hernandez

Some studies say that we sleep a third of our lives. Not just because we want to, but because our body and brain need it. I could argue the latter since I always suffer from insomnia and my body seems to work quite well. But what if we could control our dreams, like any science fiction movie where Arnold Schwarzenegger saves the world?

Can you imagine being able to decide what do you want to dream tonight? What do you want to experience today? And that all your dreams were as vivid as possible and where you could experience all those roads and paths that you never took, all those decisions and projects that you left unfinished. That relationship, that trip, that job, that career, all those possible lives, and that all your "what if ...?" had an answer. So would you live the life you currently have, or would you rather sleep all the time until you experience it all?

I would sleep all the time until I experienced it all, until I lived it all. I think I would start with my career. You know, sitting in front of a computer from 9 to 5 is not my cup of tea and sometimes I think what would have happened if I had not stopped the piano lessons that my parents forced me to take every day when I was 9 years old.

I would dream that life of concerts and tours around the world. Maybe I would've been part of an orchestra and would have a house on the beach. I would record an album or be part of the soundtrack of some famous movie, maybe a new Star Wars saga. Fate would have led me to live in Los Angeles and travel the world, to enjoy fame and fortune.

But there are also gymnastics (which I quit at 12), would I have made it to the Olympics? Perhaps I would have represented my country in the greatest sports competition in the world. I would've won medals, I would've travelled the world and advertise on television and social media ridiculous things like cereal, clothes, cell phones, medicine, etc. Whatever that pays the bills and my lifestyle. I would have been invited to prestigious events like the Met Gala and I would even meet the president. But my lifespan is short. I would have had to retire at 30 and I don't know exactly what I would do. Maybe dedicate myself to teaching or I would have become a motivational speaker, you know the kind that tells you to pursue your dreams and that people pay a lot of money for it. Maybe I would have written a book and lived off my royalties. Or maybe I would have injured myself and my career would be over, I would go back to live with my parents in a wheelchair.

What if I had dedicated myself to activism and advocacy? In this life I would have studied law and dedicated myself to defending social and environmental causes. From women's rights to the Antarctica. I would have my own association and we would march through the streets demanding rights, freedom, and a change in the law. I would visit politicians in search of support, I would recruit people with my passionate speeches, maybe I would have been thrown in jail on more than one occasion and maybe I would have joined other causes and associations. We would have artists and singers on our side. I would have become a strong opposition and power figure. An opinion leader, until one fine day during one of our multiple rallies, someone would have shot me, and I would have died. But people would remember me. I would have some mural painted on the street, maybe a statue, a documentary on Netflix, something. Or maybe like everything in this ephemeral life, my death would have been on the news for a couple of days and then, everyone would forget me.

I think this office job doesn't sound so bad anymore, right? But what would have happened if I had taken that semester abroad. Maybe I would have had more friends, broadened my mind, and learned more. I would be more independent; I would have house options to visit every summer and maybe I would have fallen in love. I would have met my future husband there. We would have fallen in love, he would have proposed to me, with that we solved the visa problem, and I would never have returned to my country again, only at Christmas to visit the family. Maybe my job would have been different (as a translator or interpreter), we would have 2 children, a dog, and a minivan. We would live in the suburbs and travel to Disney on vacation every year. I would have friends who would complain about their children and their new curtains over tea, and I would have become a boring housewife. No dreams or aspirations but with a secure future... That is until my husband's new secretary stepped into our lives and that caused a horrendous divorce. Where I would have to move to a city apartment, change school for the children and look for a job. I would be financially stressed and had no friends. I would not be in a relationship, either, until my kids went off to college, since who would want to date a single mom? I would start living into my 40s and maybe write a book. I would move somewhere with an ocean view and forget everything with my new boyfriend 10 years younger than I met on my book tour.

Speaking of love and relationships, what if I had stayed with my boyfriend from high school? In this life, although we both went to different universities, we would have maintained the relationship at a distance: daily calls, messages, comments on social media, zoom or skype every week. At every school break we would have seen each other, spent the holidays together, and even traveled. Take a few summers to work together on our theses or research projects, community service or internships. Until finally, after our graduation, we moved in together. We both would have looked for work and we would have gotten it. Of course, his job would have been better than mine. He was always smarter and more ambitious, and he is also a man, so things are easier. He would travel constantly and have annual bonuses and pay raises. I would spend all the time complaining about my job and my boss. Eventually he would take care of everything: rent and all the bills. We would adopt a pet and I would resign to dedicate myself to something else. Maybe I would have my own event planning business. With his financial support, my business would take off and become important in the city, organizing the best events. We would be one of those powerful couples without children who at any moment would take a vacation to Paris or a cruise. It would have been a good life to dream it over and over again.

But what if I had stayed with my boyfriend from college? I would have accompanied him to all his sporting events and competitions. We would have traveled a bit, maybe only within the country. He would have taken many more years to complete college, I would already be working and paying the rent and some of the bills. Their parents would help us. But eventually that would cause stress in the relationship, you know someone who is still in college and partying, while I already have work and responsibilities. We would fight frequently. Until finally he graduated and started working in something related to sports that of course does not pay a lot of money. So, this theme would be recurring in our fights, the payment of obligations would not be equitable, we could not travel or afford ourselves luxuries. All this stress would end up building up in our relationship until finally I would have the guts to end our relationship, move to another city, and start over: new job, new apartment, new friends, and maybe a new relationship. Someone I would meet at a coffee shop that I would visit every day before going to work.

Speaking of work, what if I had stayed with a boyfriend, I had during a summer job? You know that "summer love" you meet on a vacation or summer camp. In my case, he was a passionate and very handsome boy who always took his guitar everywhere. He dreamed of one day recording an album or being the opening act of a great artist. At that moment I laughed at him, but what if I had believed him and we had stayed together? We would write to each other every day and talk on the phone. Every summer that he had a tour I would accompany him. I would become his assistant or manager, make sure he was okay and had everything he wanted. I would review his contracts and the bus he would travel to. I'd keep track of the fans, make sure none of them got between us. I would no longer have gone to university, now my life would revolve around tours, festivals, concerts, and appearances. We would have gotten married in Vegas in front of Elvis. We would have crazy parties and we would have a lot of fun. We would have a cabin in the woods where he could write and compose songs. We would have several dogs and a cat. Perhaps I had adopted the hobby of photography and would dedicate myself to updating his social networks. Or maybe I would have my own gallery and sell my pictures for a lot of money. At last, I would have something for myself. Would drugs, alcohol and constant travel be a problem between us? Of course not! We would be the perfect music couple like Bon Jovi and Dorothea Hurly or like Billie Joe Armstrong and Adrienne. Another life that I would love to dream over and over again.

What would have happened if I had accepted a new job, years ago when I had the opportunity? or if I had fought more for that promotion and the company had sent me to another country to open a new branch. I would have a different apartment, one of those like the ones you see on Pinterest and that I would love to Instagram every day (would I have the time?). I would have a Carrie Bradshaw wardrobe and a new beau every weekend that I would meet in a high-end bar where I would go for a martini or a glass of wine. I would be a confident, independent, strong, and attractive woman, ready to take on the world. Nothing would stop me. I wouldn't need anyone or anything in this life because I would be enough. Loneliness wouldn't scare me, I'd have a personal stylist, a pet, and that dream vacation every year with my annual company bonus. Another life worth dreaming and living every night.

A wise person once said (or maybe it was in a movie): *"Every path is the right path. Everything could have been anything else... and it would have just as much meaning."* Maybe the life I have now is not as great as if I had made all the previous decisions, maybe I would have traveled and had fortune. I would have had love and other things, but the good thing is that I can always close my eyes and dream everything: all the possible paths, all the *"what if?"*. Live a different life every night, be someone different every night, take on a new path every night, thanks to my dreams and the power to control, would you try it?

5

A War of Hope

by Arya

A foreign virus suddenly haunts the prosperity of Humans on Planet Earth. Nations destroyed, lives lost as the various Empires and Federations along with the support of various Kingdoms launch an offensive. Succeeding in suppressing the foreign virus, humans successfully developed an elixir which would increase the chances of winning the war. Production began in haste as the rich and mighty poured in their wealth, ramping up the production time. Yet the mortal coil had always feared the unknown, thus many refused to take this unknown path of using the tactic of consuming elixir to survive. Some even termed this as using poison to satiate one's thirst. Situation started to get better day by day. But alas, that was just the peace before the real storm. The foreign virus seemed hell-bent on destroying and eradicating humans from the face of Earth as it launched an offensive by distorting its nature and cunningness. This time the attack was far more powerful and hit the arrogant human race so deeply that the previous war could very well be described as a small conflict. But humanity with an unlimited potential to adapt did not lose hope. The Empires and Federations had already made sufficient preparation for the same as their citizens were provided with elixirs, but unlike them the smaller Kingdoms which focused more on providing aid rather than catering their own citizens who feared the unknown, were hit badly.

One of those Kingdoms was Indi-o, I am a citizen of this Kingdom, and this is an episode of my war. A war to get my hands on the elixir of life for me and my loved ones. A war in which two of my sisters were recruited to fight in the frontlines for. One as a reserve soldier, one as a support soldier. A war in which I lost my loved ones. A war to re-ignite the embers of hope.

*****

4th May, 2021

As usual I began my day with a hearty breakfast prepared by my lovely mom and sending my sister off to the frontlines as a reserve soldier, but the only difference this time lay in the aura surrounding me. Fear had clutched my heart so tight that breathing seemed a bit difficult at times. It was during such times that I understood why ignorance had always been a bliss. Seconds ticked by as the sun rose above my head, while I let my soul sublimate in an alternate Universe, away from the sufferings of the mortal mind, present in real life. As I was basked, in the descending glory of the Gods and the hidden cruelty of Nature, my soul was once again dragged back into reality as an intense sense of hunger gripped my stomach. It was only then I realized that only a few hours had passed by, in contrast to the century I was immersed in that Universe. Sadly, it was not the time to return to that Universe. I had a meeting scheduled with a potential company, who seemed interested in my work. So, before the meeting I decided to have a short visit to the Dream verse. It was a nice place, I would say. But careful, the Dream verse was the origin of hallucinations ruled by the powerful yet primordial Incubus and Specters who reside in the folds of space there, hunting for their prey. One mistake and you would be trapped in the Dream verse for a long time. There exist multiple ways to counter those creatures ranging from a solid willpower to even physical discomfort. But my personal favorite was the blessings that humanity had received from the God of Music combined with the current crafting technology, along with a little help from the thing left by another Primordial entity, Chronos. The weirdest part about Dream verse was that it would rarely allow one to bring back the memories of the time spent there. Indicating that the Dream verse had hidden laws governing it. And this time to the laws prohibited the transfer of memories of my time spent there, as I returned. By now it was time for me to prepare for my meeting. I donned my garb and had a beautiful conversation. After the meeting, I laid down on my bed, basking in the golden hue of sunlight, that scattered into their inherent spectrum after passing through my patterned opaque window. Soon the sun would roll down the mountains and disappear with this light. I unknowingly turn my gaze towards the artefact hanging on the wall. This artefact was derived from the laws which the Primordial entity Chronos governed during the Age of Immemorial and right after the inception of the Universe. It indicated the moment which would decide my position in this harsh, war-torn world. To summarize, it all began when humanity discovered a mutated organism carrying a trace of foreign virus which seemed to have originated from a distant place in the Universe which the Human Civilization was not aware about. Within a matter of months this foreign virus took root within the human race, trying to distort the course of balance and doom into reality. Humanity has already been fighting this battle for a year. The inception of the fear that had clutched my heart had begun when the war started. This was "the war". A war for something more than just survival. A war for hope. In the beginning humanity put forth a solid fight. Nations were destroyed, lives were lost but humanity never lost hope. At snail's pace we were taking the lead in suppressing the foreign virus. Humanity used the one thing that they had always been proud of, their solid intellect and were able to come up with an elixir to stop the inhibition of the foreign virus. Just when we thought we were successful in pushing the virus back, it strikes us again with a newfound or maybe by using its hidden trump card. This time the target, those kingdoms who were not ready.

As a result, the casualties have been increasing lately. Unlike other empires and federations who were on the verge of winning, and possessed ample resources, my kingdom would seem small but still the subjects of my kingdom including me, were giving our all to fight this war. Brave soldiers equipped with the special equipment and took to the frontlines while others fought their battles from the safe lines. Little by little the resources within the kingdom were depleting rapidly. The citizens of my kingdom burned with fervor as they scrambled to help and provide support but still victory seemed a bit too far. I was a proud citizen of the Kingdom of Indi-o which was already running dry on resources by contributing it to the big powerful Empires and Federations scattered throughout the globe. Thus, we were running low on the stocks of elixirs required for our citizens. In the beginning, people were afraid of consuming the only source of remedy we had and after the resurgence of the enemy people were scrambling for the same. But this did not stop me. I took my artifact and connected it to the global transmission channel in order to determine the feasibility of the now scarce elixir across the kingdom. Suddenly, an intense sense of foreboding swept past my spine, and I felt my palms drenched in sweat. I nervously gulped my saliva and thought, maybe today, was the day. As my artifact connected, I was drawn into the grimoire, which was responsible for allocation of the elixir. In order to verify my identity, I entered my unique keyword, and waited for the spirit of the grimoire to send me my corresponding keyword in order to cross the enchantment barrier. After what seemed like an eternity, I felt a tinge from my artifact, the moment had arrived. Finally, the barrier had been opened. My fingers glide through the artifact, as my eyes narrow down to slits. My concentration and focus were elevated to the highest level as possible to be achieved by a mortal. Flashes of red flew past my eyes at a rapid speed, my fingers turning into a blur. Just when the list seemed to have reached an end, an unusual spark of green was reflected in my pupils. My fingers stopped their crusade as my pupils widened with joy. There it lay, the source of hope and the elixir of life. Immediately I switch to the next tactic, my body and mind as one. Punching through the required coordinates I lock onto the patch of green still shining within my eyes. In order to support my fight, my heart fought back from the clutches of fear as it increased its pace. I could feel my heart trying its best. The blood coursing through my veins. The pores on my body expanded quickly and every cell of my body absorbed the air around me causing me to suffocate with my heart pumping huge amounts of energy to my fingers and mind. An intense pang of exertion ran through my fingers as I rapidly proceeded further in the fight. There was not enough time left to even think as my instincts took over my body. Due to the exertion, I started feeling dizzy as my mind felt heavy. It was an indication that my body was on the verge of breakdown, it could not handle the intense strain. I gently bit my tongue to stay awake feeling the taste of iron in my mouth and took in a deep breath to satiate my lungs refilling them with the necessary air required by my body. Finally, I was at that moment when victory seemed to be in my grasp. The embers of hope hidden deep within seemed to be igniting in my heart. Yet my fingers were losing their strength. Hang on, just a single moment. I grit my teeth and say to myself. The final action was done and now everything was left for the spirit of the grimoire to decide whether it would be my turn or not. I had already lost all my strength. I lay there on the bed, breathing roughly, my eyes barely holding up. The embers deep within were ready to be ignited into a new spark. But alas, after what seemed like an eternity a message showed up on my artifact written in an ancient script, depicting my loss in this battle. I sigh gently and close my eyes. Resting, preparing myself for another battle, which would soon follow in the light of the moon and under the testimony of the stars. The embers of hope quietly sublimating into the body, accumulating, ready to ignite themselves once again with full glory.

6

See You in My Afterlife

by Khushi Sharma

Ever since growing up I have seen some different kinds of love, one is that we get from our mothers, one is that we get from our fathers, one is that our mother and father have and the kind of love we see in movies but there was one which was my favourite among all of these, my grandparents. I really do not know how it started, how they met, was it an arranged marriage or love. It was just as pure as the holy water and as deep as the sea, it had a different aura, a different vibe. They addressed each other respectfully, taking care of each other, crossing the road together, *Nanu* (grandpa) helping *Nani* (grandma) in the kitchen. Whenever I visited *Nani*, she never stopped talking about him, even if he was out for some work. I really wanted a relationship like them while growing up. They cared for each other, cooked for each other, even they lived for each other. I wish if I ever get married, I get as lucky as them and as compatible as them.

I have seen my *Nani's* whole world around him, it started with him and ended with him. It came more into my vision when *Nanu* got sick and all she did was take care of him and every time he recovered, she had a different spark in her eyes. She literally did miracles for him to get recover. But there was a day he did not, and left his soulmate. I know he would be up there smiling at her, getting happy when she gets happy here and crying when she cries right here. They say a human gets seven lives, if it was their first, they still are together for the rest six.

When *Nanu* left, *Nani* was left broken, he cried for hours but still could not cry her heart out, that man was her whole world. '*What would she do now?*' was my first question.

I always wondered how their love life would be back in the day, grieving for Grand-dad I really wanted to know about how their love story started. Some days passed and I still desired only one thing, to know about my grandparents and their love story.

I always believed in deities, angels, god's messenger and wishing on 11.11. Hence, every time my clock struck to 11 hours and 11 minutes, I used to wish that If I could go back in time when they got married by some time travelling thing or something.

A year passed by, and it was the death anniversary of my grandpa, my family gathered to hold a ceremony for him, it is basically *puja* in Hindus where we pray for the dead's peaceful afterlife. Unfortunately, I could not attend the ceremony because I was in college. I went to the rooftop to get some fresh air because I was devasted that a whole new life was in front of me and I could not tell him about my day and talk about my presentation or how interesting the subject pneumatics engineering and machines are, '*I wish I could tell you that I was learning a new language and how frustrating it is in college because I am always homesick.*' I just wanted to do all the granddaughter-grandfather things we did together. I was sitting on a ledge on the rooftop and thinking how that grey hair, average heighted wise old man meant so much to me. Whenever I had anything that I could not figure out I used to run to him, and he used to solve it in minutes whether it was a math problem or a real-life issue. As my leg was swinging down the ledge while I was reminiscing about my grandpa, I looked at my watch and it was 11.11 and I wished to see my grandparents together one more time, even If I can do that in my dream. After stargazing for few hours, I went back to my room and lied on my bed for a while, and I could still see the moon outside my window, and I slept gazing on the beauty of the sky full of stars and the bright moon. The next day I again went to the roof-top and wished at 11:11 again while looking at the brightest star in the sky that time. When I was coming back to my room from the roof top, I saw an old lady waiting outside my room. For once I thought it was my hostel warden, but she introduced herself as "God's messenger" She was an old, small-heighted woman wearing a greyish-blue gown, like the clouds before it's going to rain. I thought these kinds of stuffs were only present in books and series, but it was happening to me for real. When I initiated to talk to her, she already knew what was going inside my mind. *'So, you want your grandparents to meet again? Huh!'* she asked.

My jaw dropped and eyes were widened. *'How do you know?'* I asked. *'Ha-Ha-Ha I know everything my child'* she giggled. *'You have been wishing the same thing from the past one year at 11.11 hour that I had to show up.'* I could not understand her, I was about to ask her, but she already knew my thoughts and she replied without me even speaking my question, *'The angels have made a Guest house of the moon which welcomes some special guests, they come there after their death, rest, fulfil their desires and when they are ready, they proceed to their afterlife.'* She told me. I only read about these in some fictional novels, but I never knew there was something like this in real. *'My child it is real, and I am here to help you with your wish'* she said. *'Oh my god! She can read each word I am thinking.'*

'Yes, my child I know everything you are thinking'

'So, how do I believe if this all true what are you are saying' I could not believe her and hence she showed me a clip which was more like a CCTV footage but for the ghosts. It was *Nanu*, sitting at a library and he was doing some calculations which he always liked when he was alive, in his last days I remember he was devastated because his vision was blurry, and he could not do his math. I was happy he could

that there. My eyes were watery after watching him. *'Don't cry my child, he misses you all and always talks about you all.'* I hugged and asked her while sobbing when we can meet him. She said that there were rules that I must keep in mind before meeting him otherwise every alive visitor's life would get in danger. She started telling me the rule, *'The first rule is wearing a blue-coloured dress as only alive visitors wear that colour. Second rule is you can only bring one other guest along with you. Third rule is you can only visit the guest house of the Moon when it's full moon and solar eclipse on the same day. Fourth rule is you will only get 90 minutes with the person and then they will proceed to after-life. And you will have to drink a spelled tonic before visiting the guest house so that you only see the person you are signed for meeting and no other souls and after you take the exit from the guest house you will only remember it as a dream.'*

The next day I took the earliest flight to my grandma's place as the day we were supposed to see *Nanu* was after three days. She was surprised to see me at such short notice, but I did not take any more time to tell her what our plans are after three days. She was equally baffled after listening to the whole thing, but she was happy. She had happy-tears. *'I will prepare everything I wanted to feed him. I will buy him a new pair of socks and a shirt. He must look handsome before going to his afterlife.'* She started sobbing while telling me this, I was also crying watching her like that. She was so excited to see him, she was asking which saree should she drape before going to meet him. We decided a very beautiful blue silk saree with prints for her. *'It was your Nanu's favourite saree, he always complimented me whenever I wore this in front of him'*. She did her hair and put a thumb-sized tika on her forehead like she used to do before *Nanu's* death. She got ready as if it was their date, maybe it was their date but an afterlife date. It was 11:11 and I prayed again, the God's messenger came and gave us the tonic to drink. After that she asked us to close our eyes and when we opened our eyes we were there. It was the Guest house of the moon. We entered the room the messenger asked us to go and there he was, my handsome old man, my Nanu. I burst into tears after seeing him. He smiled firmly. I missed his firm smile. *'Aarti ji! You finally came to meet me',* I was so happy I could make them meet again. *Nanu* and *Nani* had a long conversation, she gifted him the shirt and sock she brought for him, and she also made his favourite dish. He ate that with so much love. *Nani* showed him the picture of our youngest cousin and said, *'See, doesn't she look like you?' 'Oh! Yes, she looks like me. Ha Ha. Now you will not miss me so much Aarti ji'* He replied. *'What rubbish Thakur ji. I always miss you.'* She spoke. Then I told him how she did not want to get ready after he was gone, *'Nanu, you know she doesn't even get ready now as she says who will compliment her now' 'Aarti ji I always loved seeing you get ready, and I will still do. Please do not leave that. I will always smile at you through wind, I will always touch you through rain and always give you my warmth through the sunrays. I will be there for you Aarti ji'* he told *Nani*. She burst into tears after hearing this and said sobbingly, *'Why did you leave me so early?' 'I feel so lonely.'*

'Because Aarti ji I saw you revolving your life around me and I wanted you to have some time for your own.' 'And You know Aarti ji how unpredictable life is, we'll meet again after your last judgement' *Nanu* explained her calmly.

'I'll see you in my afterlife.' Nani exclaimed.

'Aarti ji promise me now that you will not get weak anymore, you will keep yourself strong and you will complete all the responsibilities I left behind. You will keep doing what you loved and take care of my Dearest better half.'

'I promise!' she exclaimed.

Now it was time for him to leave. He went to a room to get ready he wore the shirt and sock *Nani* gifted him. *'Do I look good Aarti ji?'* he asked. *'Perfect'* she exclaimed. *'The sock is keeping me so warm, thank you Aarti ji, I have not felt warmth like this in my feet from a very long time.'*

I went to the God's messenger and asked if we can stay a little longer for the Good-bye, after requesting she finally agreed, and we went to the end of the pool where *Nanu* was about to take off for his afterlife. It was a shabby pool connected to a tunnel which said, *'Tunnel to afterlife.'* It was time to tell him the final Good-bye. *Nanu* hugged Nani for the last time and I touched his feet, he held my hand and said, *'Stay happy Beti'*. He left for his afterlife, and I was sure he would be the most handsome angel in the heaven. We waved him Good-bye and with the next blink we were out of that place and got up on our bed. *Nani* and I never talked about that day, if it was really a dream, we had the best dream of our lives.

7

The Guy From the Bowling Alley!

I remember seeing him at the mall, our love story is kind of like a fictional tale, love at first sight or coincidence, I still doubt. He caught my eyes. He had a different personality, which separated him from the rest of the crowd.

It was my day off, so my friends and I decided to hang-out at the nearest mall, we were bowling soon afterwards my eyes got stuck on someone. That boy was standing there with his friends waiting for his turn for bowling and I was standing there trying to take my eyes off him. Huh! It was something about his personality that did not let me take my eyes off him and every time he looked at me, I used to look somewhere else. He was wearing a face mask but even from that distance I saw his pretty eyes, I was curious I really wanted to know the person behind those eyes. Our game was over, but I did not want to leave so soon, I wanted to go talk to him, but I did not have the guts to do that. We came out of the gaming zone and him and his friends went to the same slot we left. Well! That was a coincident...I was wearing my shoes and my friends were sitting there bragging about who played the best and I was there looking at the TV screen to get his name while acting up as if I was tying my laces. Well, I waited there to see his name and let my friends tease me for losing the game. I was least interested in them. I just wanted his name, and I got it Yay! his name was quite intriguing like his personality. The first thing I did was searched him on Instagram, but I could not find his handle by just knowing his first name. I wish I had some courage to at least ask him his Instagram handle.

After a month of that incident, I was swiping right and left on some random dating app, and I saw him again. We matched! I took it as a sign from my Guardian angel. This time I really did not want him to let go so I searched him on Instagram, and I found him. Hurray! I instantly texted him the whole bowling incident and we started to talk. I really thought he would be mean because c'mon he was so handsome; he might have got a lot of texts like mine. But eventually into the conversation he turned out to be the sweetest guy I ever talked to. After a week we went to our first date and after three dates we started dating, it all felt like a dream as if I was dating some guy from my fantasy. All of this was so sudden, but our vibes completely matched. We connected on a different level as if we knew each other from somewhere but both of us had no idea where?

It was two months of dating already; he was returning from a trip, and I went to receive him from the airport. He was exhausted and sleep deprived so I asked him to rest at my place for a while. We finally reached at my place and ordered some food and switched on the AC and we sat down on the bed. I asked him to lie down, he was tired and was sleep deprived. He came and lied down on my lap. That was sweet, he looked so comfortable, like a child. I caressed his head and made him comfortable.

When he woke up and talked a little about his trip, he even got me a gift. I was so happy and awed. He really cared about me. It was such a cute gesture. After that, he kissed me on my forehead. I looked at him and asked him to kiss me on my eyes, then nose and then my neck, we looked at each other for a while then we started kissing. We smiled at each other, and he cuddled me like a teddy bear, rested a leg on mine and rested his head on the pillow while mine was on my handy pillow, his shoulder. We were talking about something, and he kissed me again on my forehead and said, *'I Love you my world'*. I kissed him on his lips and said, *'I love you too'* and, we started kissing again but this was something different, it was more passionate, and it was like all we wanted that time was each other. I moved back slowly, and he crawled over me following the movement, now he was on top of me kissing my neck, I lifted his T-shirt a little while kissing him and he took it off, damn! his physique I was amazed, I touched him a little, but he came onto me again and started kissing me. He gazed his eyes upon me for a bit and started kissing me again, he went down to kiss me, he slipped down to my belly and started kissing it slowly coming upwards, it was so fascinating I cannot even explain. I literally had Goosebumps. He started kissing my neck and I was lying there hugging him tight and tighter towards me, my breaths were heavy, I never thought this could be us. He was tender and firm but passionate. *'What if I ask you something inappropriate?'* He knew what I meant; he replied in the cutest way possible, *'We still aren't ready.'* May be that is what I wanted to hear, he remembered my past insecurities, and that made me feel stronger for him. I knew I love the right person. We cuddled for a while and he rested his head on my shoulder looking like a kid, so adorable then he tucked me in and rolled to the other side, while my head was on his shoulder, I heard his heartbeat and it was for sure not normal, *'Why is your heart beating so fast?'* I asked *'it's *pause* you'* he replied. I kissed him and we both slept for a while, he was watching me sleep and smiling, he was tracing my eyes with his finger, caressing my head softly, tapping my back to make me sleep, I opened my eyes for a second and saw him sleeping so peacefully. *'I love you'* my heart said. When we woke-up we decided to go out, so we got dressed and went out to eat and shop. I wore his tee I liked a lot and apparently stole that too I was jumping around in his tee, and he was looking at me while I was jumping around like a kid, watching me as if he was overwhelmed while I was brushing my hair, smiling when I asked him how was I looking in his tee and replying with just a word '*perfect*,' all of those actions were so adorable. He tried to hide all of those, but I knew what he was feeling. So, we roamed and shopped a lot. Lol!

After we came back home, we sat down drank some water and he started packing, watching him pack made me sad, I didn't want him to go so soon. I was devasted and he saw that, so he came and hug me and lifted me up and swung me round like I was a doll. Well! I am, his doll.

I went to drop him in the evening, hugged him and gave him a peck on the cheeks. My eyes were a little numb, I didn't want the day to end. All I wanted was him by my side forever like that.

I came home and I was already exhausted, so I changed to my night-suit and went to sleep when at midnight I heard a knock on my window. I was really scared and then my phone started ringing, it was him, I sighed and picked up his call, '*Babe! someone is knocking at my window*.' I told him nervously. '*Princess that's me*' he replied. I opened the window, and it was really him, I sneaked him in and hugged him so tight as if I would not let him go anywhere the next time. '*Were you missing me Princess?*' he asked. '*Of-course I was missing you, You duffer!*'

'*I am here kiddo*' I pulled him closer, he was on me and took off his shirt and mine in one stroke. '*I think we are ready now*' he exclaimed. He was all over me, kissing every inch of my body and in the next second my hands were on his pants, he came up and kissed my neck. He was going down slowly kissing my stomach and reached the lower abdomen. He slowly started sliding down my panties and was kissing each part that was revealing inch by inch simultaneously. I screamed his name and I think that was exciting for him. He started using his finger on my vagina. I grabbed his hair then loosened my grip and started caressing his head with my fingers between his hair. He came up, kissed me on my lips, slowly moved down and started kissing every part of my body. I returned the favour and started kissing him passionately, then his neck, repeating his movements and slid down to his chest and then his stomach, his lower abdomen and removed his trousers. I gave him a head, he closed his eyes and held all my hair behind, he turned me around and slightly pushed it. I moaned out loud, he came closer and kissed me and asked, *'Are you okay princess?'*

'Never been better before' I replied in a squeaky voice, he pushed it in deeper and started kissing me harder on the neck, on the shoulders. *sighs* I bit his shoulder to lower my moans. He was kissing my neck at that time and rubbing on my clitoris simultaneously, damn it was so hot.

I heard my phone ringing I went to see who that was, when I saw my phone I was shocked. It was him *'Hello'* *panting* *'Babe are you okay, why are you panting and sweating so much'* he asked.

'It was just a dream, never mind.'

The dream was wild, yet he knew what was his even in the dream.

You know the feeling when you are hundred percent sure about how your partner feels for you, I had the same feeling. He loves me like it's still our first day of dating, he handles my panic attacks, he feeds me, and he never complains about anything. It was already a year of us dating now and our bond was getting stronger each day.

One fine I found a diary in my drawer, but it was weird because it was from ten years ahead of the present year. When I opened it and started reading it, I read something I could have never imagined.

'Huh! I cannot imagine it's finally happening; I cannot imagine I am finally wearing the white gown I always wanted to wear. I don't know how will he react? Will he cry? Will he hug me? I don't know! I just hope everything goes well and I do not get stuck in my veil. I am thinking how will I read the vow in front of him. God! I am finally getting married to him and on the same day we first went on a date. I am finally getting married to my prettiest dream. My angels bless me!'

When I read this, I was shocked, whom did I marry? Was it him really? So, we'll really end up getting married? I wanted to read what happened after that and what was written on my vow.

Hence, I turned the page, and it was written, '*My prettiest dream, when we first met at the bowling alley, I did not know we would come this far, standing in front of each other and the whole family to read our vows. I just cannot tell you how much I love you and how lucky I feel to have you by my side. Your eyes are the prettiest, it always says the truth and......*' *Knock Knock*

My mother knocked at the door, and I hid the diary in that drawer. The next morning when I came to read the next page of the diary it was gone. I could not find it anywhere in the room. I was clueless if that diary was real, or I saw a dream again.

8

The Champa Tree

Debjyoti Das

The fairies still come and sit on the branches of the Champa tree in full moon nights.

In herd they come like fireflies and transform the moonlit garden into a fairyland.

It is a hypnotic spectacle that turns Rishi into a stupor, a state of physical and mental inertness. As if intoxicated, he indulges himself to enjoy the most beautiful vision of his life during the winter and the spring seasons of the year, when the garden is in full bloom with various radiant flowers. The pool beside the garden becomes lively reflecting the moonbeams as the calm yet agitated water starts the prelude of the arrival of the fairies. Among the array of lights, stands the Champa tree, with white-yellow flowers.

The strong fragrance of the flowers not only attracts the insects who are simply tricked, for the flowers do not hold nectar, but also lures Rishi like a sphinx moth. As the poet Keats experienced by the song of the nightingale; Rishi feels the same drowsy numbness by the intoxicating aroma of the Champa flowers. Sitting under the moonbeams, he watches the fairies fly around the tree and among the flowers of the garden.

Rishi had seen his father taking care of the flowering plants in the garden for hours during his boyhood days. Gardening was his father's favourite hobby. With three dozen rose plants that bloomed in all seasons and especially during winter and spring, more flowering plants that made the garden a treasured rendezvous for a rainbow-coloured butterflies, dragonflies, and twittering birds. Rishi learnt the names of those flowering plants, either English or Indian names, like rose, dahlia, zinnia, chandramallika, putulika and many others. During weekends, his father used to spend the mornings and afternoons tending all the flowering plants to grow perfectly and produce big flowers in large quantities in winter and spring, when the front courtyard of their house lightened up in various blossoming hues. Some flowering trees were also present at the boundary of the garden that bloomed white and pink flowers whose name Rishi cannot remember now. Among those trees, the Champa tree was very favourite to Rishi. He simply loved the fragrance that attracted him the most. He also liked to sit on a branch at the bottom near the ground as the strong aroma of the flowers lingering in the air made him dizzy.

As a boy, he felt himself as an Aztec king sitting on his throne in the garden surrounded by his flowering noblemen.

Rishi observed how his father was engrossed taking care of the flowering plants.

While working, it seemed he was talking and smiling with the plants and the flowers now and then. At night his father walked between the rows of flowers with a joyous expression on his face, praising his own creation. The fragrance of the flowers wafting across every corner of the garden transformed into a paradise for him. The perfume of the Champa flowers enriched the aroma, mixing with others and converted the surroundings into a heavenly abode. Rishi's father as if like Lord Krishna strolling down his heavenly abode enjoying the beauty of his sacred garden. The flowers transformed into his consorts joyously welcoming him to singing and dancing.

Once Rishi's grandmother picked up some roses from the garden and offered them to the God, while Rishi's father was in office. When he returned in the evening and while entering he noticed the missing roses in the garden. Without a word he went straight into the house and found them in front of the photo of the God. He simply took the photo and threw them outside and declared that the flowers were naturally beautiful in his garden, and he didn't want that God for whom the beauty of his garden would be lost.

Apparently, the action of throwing away the God's picture by his father seemed strange and cruel to Rishi, but he was pondering more over the words his father had spoken. That day he realised the idea of true beauty and thus framed his mind to find out the original beauty which is the truth. Later, one day he asked his uncle and aunt who was devout Vaishnava, whether they would offer the expensive delicacies to God every day before having themselves, if God would really have them. He didn't get back the answer, but he was labelled as an atheist for his question.

The immediate neighbour of Rishi's family was a famous tea-merchant of Calcutta. They owned some tea gardens in North Bengal and Assam and had a number of tea shops around the city. Their flourishing business helped them to become one of the richest business families in Calcutta. They had a big farmhouse and was said that the farmhouse was once belonged to an Englishman who sold it to a famous lady writer.

Later the tea-merchant bought it from her. Being rich they had renovated the farmhouse into a wonderful place with an aviary, a cowshed, some vegetable, and flower gardens.

They had kept a chimpanzee, as a pet, that used to sit on top of the boundary wall beside Rishi's house. Although Rishi couldn't have the opportunity to meet with the ape for it died when he was two years old. All these facts of that family, he had heard from his mother later. But Rishi was lucky to have clicked a photo with two tiger cubs that the family had kept for some time, having caught them in their tea estate in North Bengal.

The family also had the glory of having their name among the first listed customers who related to Calcutta Telephone lines in the city.

Rishi had a childhood playing partner in that tea-merchant's house, a girl, two years older than him. Her name was "Japi" evidently her name suggests her look as fair as the Japanese. It was a routine affair for him to climb the wall and jump into the compound of the farmhouse to play with her. While playing one day, Rishi discovered a

Champa tree at the back of their house. Till then he knew that the Champa flowers were white with yellow in the middle. But the mesmerizing smell attracted him to discover the tree, but the colour of the flowers was hot pink, which made him aware the diverse beauty present in nature around him.

His realisation transferred him to a dreamy island, a dreamy Polynesian island of Hawaii, where he with his partner, amorously intoxicated, dancing around the Champa or locally called frangipani tree, wearing a lei, or garland of "Pua Melia", as the Hawaiians called the flowers, around their neck and as head adornments. They danced round and round for hours, frequently embracing each other, exchanging sweet kisses, drunk by their charms, until they felt exhausted. Love flowed so naturally and silently that their innocent hearts only shared it without realising.

Time always shows its true colour through transformation, unveiling the harsh realities, not only for Rishi, who was approaching his teens but for all of them with whom he shared the sweet moments of his life till then.

One of the paternal aunts of Rishi who was a widow and was economically poor, eventually had a change of her destiny. Earlier she was helped by Rishi's father and her other brothers to run her family with her kids. After a long struggle, her son became highly educated and secured a job in the USA, and took his mother with him. After returning from the States, Rishi noticed his aunt's transformed look, highly acceptable now among the groups of relatives of their family for her newly achieved high economic status. When Rishi approached to touch her feet to show respect, his aunt caught his hand and with a radiant smile, extended her right hand for a handshake and then hugged him affectionately.

Rishi was fascinated by the gesture of her aunt. While embracing her, he was aware of a smell of a perfume which always attracted and made him hypnotized, the same aroma of Champa flowers. Awestruck he kept on staring at his aunt. The lady whom he had earlier seen wearing a cheap white cotton saree, withered and old, suddenly transformed into a blooming flower, clad in a cream-white silk saree with full of gold ornaments on her body. She was as if a gorgeously bloomed Champa flower, mesmerizing and exhilarating. On the grave of her old, withered past stood the newly born Champa tree, with full of blossoms, staring and smiling at him, bright and pure, standing before his eyes, as if a heavenly damsel in the frescoes of the fifth-century Sigiriya rock fortress of Sri Lanka. Distracted, Rishi's mind wandered through the vast unknown historical land of fantasy in the remote past.

Sometimes, harsh reality also leads us to fantastic dream to escape from the trials and complexities of our lives. For Rishi, his teenage mind was trying to find the balance between the emotional and rational side of his life, somewhat a roller-coaster ride, up to a fantasy of imagination and suddenly down to the ground realities.

Trials and tribulations appear suddenly unnoticed. The death of the tea-merchant led to a long-drawn legal battles among his sons and relatives. One by one, the tea-estates and the shops were sold. The downfall of their fortunes began. The farmhouse turned into a little forest, where snakes and jackals made their hideouts. At night the jackals and the owls started their nightly concert. Even the jackals came into the garden of Rishi's father and their cubs came out at dusk to play their mischievous games like puppies. Rishi liked to watch them but dared to go close. But the most fascinating scene always waited for Rishi was during the full moon nights.

The forested part of the farmhouse became the backdrop at the eastern side of the garden. As the evening darkness enveloped the surroundings, the moon came out behind the forest, the dark trees silhouetted against the moonlight, the garden transformed into a moonlit paradise. Basking in the pale golden moonbeams, Rishi silently savoured the 'moonlight sonata' for hours, inebriated by the sight and smell of the garden. Overwhelmed by the magical spell, he watched the heard of fairies flying around the garden and sat on the branches of the Champa tree. A radiant glow encircled the Champa tree forming a halo around it. The aroma of the flowers was lingering in the air. Rishi breathed heavily; his head felt heavy. He felt dizzy by the illusive spectacle.

He closed his eyes and dreamed the moonlit garden, the Champa tree and the flying fairies. He could see himself then, playing around the tree with them. Surprisingly, he noticed his playing mate, a girl of his age, standing among the fairies. She smiled at him, enticingly and extended her arms towards him, inviting to join her. Enchanted by her invitation, Rishi felt a familiarity in her, but he could not recognize her.

Reality robbed of fairies when he stepped out of his teenage. His mother died of heart ailment, leaving his father alone who developed schizophrenia attacks and five years later, he also expired. The garden gradually lost its glory having missed their careful master. The municipal corporation of the town took over the pool which dried up and converted it into a public park. In the process, the Champa tree faded into oblivion.

The forested part of the land of the neighbouring tea-merchant was sold after solving the pending legal battles and a huge multi-storied complex came up.

Rishi is too busy now to observe these changes as he has the burden to maintain his family, having married after his parents' death. The fast-changing market economy system of the country has hit him so hard that he has been compelled to dismantle his dilapidated ancestral house and offered the land to develop into a multi-storied complex.

Eventually, the dream heaven of his childhood vanished to obscurity.

But still, the full moon nights usher him to join with the fairies who come and sit on the imaginary Champa tree for him. He can see himself, a boy who happily plays around the tree with his playing mate. He stops frequently to take a deep breath to fill up his heart with the intense fragrance of the Champa flowers that bloom gorgeously. Drunk by the aroma, the vision gives him immense pleasure and his favourite haunt to escape from the crude reality momentarily. The obscure Champa tree is now among one of his essential earthly existences and identities.

9

Show Me What I Am

by Aanika G

Her head throbbed as she heard laughs around her. *'Do our homework for us, or else, you know!'* Saanvi warned. She fell to the ground as her enemy kicked her stomach and walked away. *'You better give it by the lunch break.'* Rekha said in a sing-song voice, kicking her left shoulder. She felt the world go blurry as her eyes shut.

'Why are you late, Amaira?' Her math teacher asked when she entered the classroom.

'S-sorry sir, I had a stomach ache!' she stuttered.

'Lies. All lies. Stand near the board.' Amaira sighed and nodded. This was the fifth time in the week she got scolded, for something she didn't do. She looked at Saanvi and Rekha, who tried to hold their laughter. *'What are you doing?'* her teacher asked, when she was not coming to the spot, he asked her to.

'Oh, Amy, I'm really sorry for the trouble I caused you.' Saanvi whispered mockingly when she nears them. She threw her bag on her table- which was in front of Saanvi's and Rekha's, unfortunately- in frustration and cringe at the nickname. *'Behave, Amaira. Stand outside the class.'* Her teacher ordered. At this point, she felt like crying. She could do nothing but listen to the snickers of the people she hated the most.

'Your principal called. He said you were rude to your Chemistry teacher. This is the second time this week, Amaira.' Her mother said when she came back from school. Amaira groaned, plopping on the couch. *'You were such a good child, what happened to you? We pay the fees for you to misbehave?'*

'Mom, leave me alone, please!' Amaira replied.

'Am' She let out a loud shout, interrupting her mother. She ran up the stairs and into her room, shutting the door with force. Leaving her mother in shock. She immediately burst into tears.

'Why does everyone treat me like that? Am I really that bad?' She spoke to herself, looking at the full-length mirror in front of her bed. *'I guess it's because I'm fat.'* She held her waist. *'And ugly.'* she added, wiping the tears from her cheeks. She thought she saw the reflection in the mirror blink, when she was aware she wasn't blinking. But she shrugged the thought and threw herself on the bed, kicking her legs in irritation. She eventually fell asleep.

Rubbing her puffy eyes, she found the time to be 7:30 in the evening. *'Start doing your math homework.'* She ignored the voice in her head. *'I said do your math homework.'*

'There's no use, I'm not going to school ever.' She fought back to her mind.

'Do not be ridiculous, go. Do it.' Regardless, Amaira took out her phone. Within seconds she put it back down and proceeded to walk to her table. *'What am I doing? I'm not going to attend school.'* She thought to herself.

'You were being stubborn. I had to take control!' the mind said as if it had a voice of its own. She started doing her homework, and to her surprise, she knew every sum. But that couldn't be possible because she hated math. And she was awful at it.

'Amaira!' her mother called out, knocking lightly on her door. *'Come for dinner, sweetheart. I'm sorry for shouting at you.'*

Amaira's red face soon turned to a soft one as she replied, *'Yes mom, coming.'* Her mother let out a gasp in shock.

'What the heck is wrong with me?' Amaira asked herself, hitting her head multiple times. *'Hitting it won't do anything. You will only harm your head.'*

'Who are you? Get out! I don't want to eat!' She shouted to her head. Anyone near her would think she is a psychopath. She waited for her brain to respond like it did before but to no avail. *'Are you alive?'* She asked it. No reply. *'Huh. Thank God!'* She slept on the bed with a sigh.

'Amaira! Come on, the food will get cold!' Her mother said.

'I'm sick of my name being used so much now.' Amaira mumbled and shut her eyes, not caring to respond to her mother. She looked at her legs as they got out of bed and started walking towards the door. *'What? Stop, stop walking. Do not move.'* She scolded her legs, hitting them to make them stop. The legs didn't listen and continued to walk as if they had a mind of their own. They walked until she forced them down. She only fell on the stairs with a loud thud, causing her mother to look up in alarm.

'Ugh, you're so stiff-necked.'

'So you're not dead.' She said out loud.

'Who's not dead?' Her mother questioned. Amaira shook her head and climbed down like nothing happened when she was burning from embarrassment inside.

'You're doing something good for once.' The voice in her brain observed as she picked the piece of bottle gourd from the plate. Just hearing the voice made her change her decision. She immediately put the piece down, to which the voice spoke, *'You are such a birdbrain.'*

She scoffed and answered, this time making sure she didn't say it aloud, *'Look who's talking about brains.'*

'Shut up, I'm not your brain. I'm just inside it.'

'Who are you? A ghost who invades people's brains? Get out of my brain.' She thought to herself. She felt stupid arguing with her brain, or at least someone in her brain, like the voice claimed.

'I'm you. Just better. I'm perfect.'

'I'm you. Just better. I'm perfect.' She mimicked the voice. She found her hand reaching for the glass of water which soon splashed on her face.

'What was that for?' She asked the voice but got no reply.

'You okay, honey?' Her mother looked concerned.

'Yeah, yes I am. I'm fine.' she breathed. She just nodded and went to wash the dishes. Amaira went back to her room.

'It's time you show yourself, ghost in my brain.' She said once she closed the door to her room. She didn't get a reply. *'Hello? You don't speak when I ask you to.'*

'Go to the mirror!' she heard the voice say.

She did as she was told. She knew it wasn't her reflection in the mirror. She was a lot slimmer, and a lot prettier too. The voice wasn't lying when it had said it was perfect. The reflection truly was. That explained the blinking of her reflection earlier. *'Who are you?'* Amaira whispered, touching the mirror with her soft hands. *'I told you, I'm a better version of you.'* the reflection replied. The mirror didn't act like one. It was like it had been turned to a window. The reflection was moving around while Amaira simply stood there. Suddenly she felt a sharp throb in her head, the world went white for a second. Then it was back to normal again. *'I'm back.'* Her brain said.

'Get out! I don't want a mirror reflection inside my mind.'

'Aren't you tired of being the one everyone always scolds? Aren't you? Don't you want to be known as the perfect one? Why does it have to be Saanvi or Rekha?' the voice spoke. Now that she thought about it, Amaira did want a normal life where everyone treated her well. She

nodded unconsciously.

'Good! Then let me take over you. Let me control you and make you the one everyone likes.'

'Okay.' Amaira watched as her legs took her to bed. She instantly fell asleep.

She woke up with a splitting headache. *'Amaira, you're up yet? You have school today, remember?'* Her mother shouted from outside the room.

'Mom, I don't want to g-... Um! I will wake up, mom.' she said. Her mother was surprised, and so was she. Until she remembered she had someone living in her brain.

She got out of bed with a light head, dreading to go to school. But her ego took over. She wanted to become the best.

'Bye mom, I'm leaving!' she said, holding a slice of bread in her mouth.

She walked to school with a clear mind, knowing that her perfect self will correct her.

And it did. She improved in drawing (which she was bad at, just like any other subject), sports and she also argued back to Saanvi and Rekha. Which she never dared to do. Her classmates started to accept her as one of their own, they even included her in the Truth or Dare game they always played. But Saanvi and Rekha hated this new form of hers. Perhaps because they were jealous. They tried to harm her more. (Keyword- "tried". Amaira only held them back with the strength she had.)

This continued for two weeks, and everyone seemed to be fond of her.

Amaira sat at her study table- her body in her room, her mind someplace else. *'You are being stubborn again. One minute I stop controlling you and you're already somewhere else.'*

'You just love the word stubborn, don't you?' She asked her brain.

'I love it when I'm the one calling you stubborn. Forget that. I think it's finally time for you to control yourself. I've stayed long enough now and trust me, your nerves stink.'

'You can smell my nerves? That's disgusting.' she hissed.

'Not the point. I mean half the point but NOT the point.' the voice said.

'Well then what's the point?'

'I want you to be you. Not me.'

'You do realize we're technically the same, right?'

'We aren't, actually. I'm the better version.' Amaira groaned at that.

'Yeah, yeah, Miss perfect.' She rolled her eyes.

'It's time for me to leave your mind.' The voice insisted.

'But people are so nice to me. They will hate me if I turn back to normal again. I can't lose you. It's like saying Superman lost his ability to fight.'

'So you used me? I was just a way to get people to like you?' The voice angered.

'Wasn't that why you invaded my brain in the first place?'

'I wanted a friend, Amaira. Believe me, this might sound stupid, but being locked up in a mirror is not fun. You know what, forget it. I'll be in your mind for how much every time you want. You're my "master" after all.' She enraged. Amaira didn't speak as guilt took over her.

Amaira knew she didn't feel like herself. She knew she wasn't the one gaining the courage to do everything. *'Hey,'* she whispered to her head when she was in the washroom at school the next day.

'Miss perfect, you there?' She tapped her head. The voice in her head hummed in response.

'As much of an arrogant little witch you are, I'm thankful to you. You

made me realise that with just a little courage I could completely change what people, except for those two brats.' At this point, she didn't care about the looks people shot her as they passed by her talking to herself. *'I don't think I need you anymore. I'm sorry for yesterday, I shouldn't have used you like that. I'll be good from now and I'll make sure you don't get in my brain again. Feel free to talk to me from the mirrors.'*

'Aww, but it's hardly been a month. I enjoyed controlling you.'

Amaira chuckled. *'I question your mood changes. Come out.'* she said.

Her head throbbed once more until she opened her eyes and looked at the mirror in front of her. *'Thank you again.'*

The mirror self-waved at her. *'Go!'* Amaira said impatiently when the mirror self wouldn't stop waving.

'Geez, okay. But seriously, I'm proud of you. Until next time, then!' The reflection replied and disappeared, leaving Amaira to look at her imperfect self. *'I like me.'* she declared. *'No, I love me!'* She walked out of the washroom with pride. No one even noticed the difference in her attitude. She was her perfect self.

10

The Chase

by Aanika G

"Good job, Dhruth!" His coach told him as Dhruth felt him patting his back. *"If you practice a little more, I'm sure you'll come first in the competition. You're already the best in the district."*

He crossed the road carefully, gripping onto his white cane. He was on his way to his boarding school from his favourite cafe. He felt exhausted after a good four hours of running. He loved to run from when he was a child. The fact that he was blind didn't stop him. He was practising for his state-level sprint competition. Entering his room to rest, he immediately drifted off to deep sleep.

Suddenly he woke to loud sirens inside the building. He could hear people outside shouting, *'Fire emergency! Evacuate the building!'* He got up and started running towards the stairs to leave the building and saw people pacing side to side. After a lot of getting pushed around in between people, he finally got to take a good look at the building. He watched in fear as the fire engulfed the building, and firemen rushed around, trying to diffuse the fire. He noticed a blind person on the roads, whom he guessed to be from the boarding school, struggling to cross it. Dhruth picked his stick up and guided him to the other side, like any person helping a blind man. It was at that time that he noticed he could see. That left the lad wondering how it was possible. He felt a tap on his back and turned to see a man in beach shorts and a loose white t-shirt. He was pleasantly surprised at his choice of clothing during a weekday. The man looked so relaxed, no one could tell he was standing in front of a building on fire. His white beard cascaded down his chest, slightly curled in the end. He wore a red cap on his head, sea-blue eyes shining from under his spectacles. *'Care to have pizza with me?'* He asked, staring into his eyes. He was so manipulative that Dhruth couldn't say no. Plus, it usually meant they would pay when an elderly was treating a younger one. Who would reject free pizza? He nodded and followed the man as if in trance. Dhruth looked at the building, which was now black of smoke. The firemen continued to put out the fire.

The man walked to the cafe in front of the burning building. Dhruth quickly recognized it to be his favourite cafe. Now that he could see, he noticed no other cafe near the place. *'That's why the cafe was so crowded.'* he thought to himself. Even though he ate before he slept, looking at the pizzas on the menu made his stomach grumble. Which was weird because he never ate much.

He was mesmerized by the view inside the cafe. Chains of fairy lights decorated the walls, polaroid of the customers stuck in some places. A chandelier hung from the ceiling. The man sat on a chair, gesturing Dhruth to sit in front of him. He played with the tiny plant in front of him. *'So, this is what a plant looks like.'* he thought.

'The fire was all of a sudden, do you know why that happened?' The man asked. Before Dhruth could speak, the man continued, *'You had a good sleep?'* Dhruth nodded, asking him the same question. *'Ah, yes. I even got a dream that felt so real. I think I was talking in my sleep too.'* The man laughed, even his laugh felt pleasing to Dhruth. *'Dreams are much more real than the real world, aren't they?'* He spoke again. Dhruth simply nodded again. *'My dream ended abruptly. I might just go and continue it after everything settles.'* the man said.

'How can you do that?' Dhruth seemed intrigued. The man let out a small chuckle again. *'I just remember what happened.the last in my*

dream before going to sleep. Then I let my mind do the rest.' Suddenly Dhruth felt someone hit his head from behind. Before he could see who, it is, he collapsed on the ground.

He groaned and massaged his head. He could not see anything. By the smell and sounds coming from outside, he recognized it to be his dorm room. *'So, it was all a dream.'* he muttered to himself. *'I wanted that pizza though.'* He tutted and stood up. He found it strange how he could see in his dream and not in reality. He wondered if he had got that kind of dream because of his fear of fire. It was because of fire that he lost his sight, after all. When he was just a toddler. He wondered if the man in beach shorts did something to him to get his sight back in the dream. You couldn't blame him for thinking that way, anyone would get attracted to the man. Like how people agree with everything their favourite idol says, or like the man was a mind controller.

He couldn't stop thinking about his dream the whole day, even when he practiced running. The coach even scolded him for not concentrating. But Dhruth was too occupied in his thoughts. He wanted to have a dream where he can see again. He wanted to meet the eerie yet peaceful man again. He thought about everything they spoke about, trying to remember every detail. That's when he remembered what the man had talked about sleeping again and getting the same dream. *'I must try it.'* he muttered to himself. *'Let me grab some pizza before I go, the pizza in my dream has caused me to crave for it.'* He went to the cafe again. The owners were familiar with him by this time, he visited very often. *'Can I have a Margherita, please?'* He heard a voice say. The voice aroused Dhruth. He never thought he would be attracted to someone by their voice. Disregarding the thought, he satisfied himself by eating and walked to his room. After a lot of turning around on his bed, he finally fell asleep. He didn't forget to remember what had happened in his previous dream before going to sleep. He just thought of the strange dude.

He was in the same cafe as before, just the man wasn't in front of him. He saw the fire trucks parked in front of the cafe and decided to get a glimpse of the now burnt boarding school of his. *'Quite an obnoxious sight, eh?'* He heard someone say. A boy of around his age stood next to him. Dhruth was sure he had heard the voice before; he just couldn't recognize the owner. The boy had sea-blue eyes that Dhruth swore he had seen before. *'Yeah!'* he replied softly. *'You live there, don't you?'* The boy asked him. Dhruth nodded.

'I do too. Atharv. Nice to meet you.' he said, extending his hand for a shake. Dhruth took it and smiled at him. *'I'm Dhruth. Where-?'* he got interrupted by a girl crying for help.

'Why is everyone's voice sounding similar to me?' He sighed.

'Excuse me please.' Dhruth said to Atharv as he walked over and asked what the matter was. *'My dog- he's still in the building! He-'* Dhruth started walking towards the building without letting her continue. He knew the building even with his eyes closed. He heard yelps coming from a room- his room. He saw the dog stuck between his desks when he ran to his room. Slowly picked the dog up, Dhruth examined the injury on its leg, quickly wrapping a piece of cloth around it.

'Thank you so much!' The girl said when he finally came down and handed the dog to her. She had hazel eyes that went perfectly with her cinnamon-brown hair. Dhruth couldn't get his eyes off her. Then he remembered where he had heard the voice- it was at the cafe, the same voice that had attracted him. *'My poor dog hurt his leg.'* she said softly to herself as she walked away. Dhruth wondered why there was a dog in a boarding school. He watched as the girl's figure disappeared.

To his surprise, the girl soon returned and gave him a pile of money as a gratitude gift.

'It's the least I can do, please take it.'

'I couldn't let a dog alone, it's the least I could do, don't worry.' He replied.

'I still need to repay you somehow, tell me how I can.'

'I don't want anything.' Dhruth smiled.

'Please!' she begged.

'What's your name?' He asked her.

'Idika.'

'Hi Idika, I'm Dhruth. Would you like to have pizza with me?' Dhruth asked without thinking. For some reason, he was getting hungrier every hour.

'Sure!' she gave him a genuine smile before leading the way.

'One Margherita, please.' she said to the waiter. *'Why would you-what's so funny?'* She asked when she saw Dhruth giggling to himself. *'Oh! Nothing.'* he answered with a straight face, laughing at her love for Margheritas. She frowned at him. *'I would like to have a veggie pizza, please.'* he said to the waiter who nodded and walked away.

'I heard you here yesterday.' he told her.

'Really? Only heard?' She tilted her head.

'Um, well, yeah.' He didn't want to tell her he was blind. He felt she would walk away from him. 'How didn't I notice you?' She asked. He shrugged, keeping his head low.

'Oh, I have a sprint competition next week, it would be great to have you there.' He lit up every time he spoke about running.

'You're in the competition? Oh my god, I love watching those!' She exclaimed, which excited Dhruth more. They continued to speak for a while until Idika's parents called and she had to go. *'I'll be there cheering for you next week!'* She chirped and waved at him after exchanging numbers. She thanked him again for saving her dog, whose name was apparently Oscar. She said she kept the name so because if she wasn't successful in the future and didn't get an Oscar award, she could still say she has Oscar. He smiled to himself and got up to walk out too until he felt himself being shaken continuously. He

shut his eyes. When he opened them, he could see nothing. *'Dhruth!'* His friend shouted. He realised he was in his dorm room. He was so into his dream that he forgot it was one. He wondered if Idika would still come to the competition. *'No, it was just a dream.'* he reminded himself, erasing his thoughts. It made him disappointed. He would still search for her in the field on the day. *'But the dream was just my imagination, how do I know if she looks the same?'* He sighed. Because of the voice he had heard first in the cafe, his evil mind had created an image and name for the voice. Now he couldn't get her face out of his mind. He cursed at his mind repeatedly.

'Finally you're awake!' his friend said. Dhruth felt him hold a sound horn and raised an eyebrow. *'I tried to wake you up a lot. You were asleep for two days. I was genuinely concerned. Even coach tried to wake you up and asked me to check on you, multiple times.'* he said to Dhruth.

'That would've been embarrassing.' Dhruth said to them, knowing his coach didn't care for them until they were running well and making him proud. He never cared if they overslept.

'It was.' his friend chuckled. *'Come on now, coach would kill me if he knew you're awake without going for practice.'* Dhruth nodded and got out of bed.

'Dude, you were sleeping like the guy in Ramayana. Ravana's brother.' His friend nudged him as they walked to the ground.

'Kumbh Karan?' Dhruth chuckled.

'Yeah! him.' The mystery of his dreams was left unsolved as he decided to try again that night.

11

The Price

by Kai Jennings

Right before I was turned into a shadow, a living shadow who existed in the space between the worlds, I heard him shouting. *'You can't do this, you promised you wouldn't do it. You idiot! I love you!'* He loved me? He seemed to be surprised that he said that, looking at me wide-eyed. *'I love you too.'* I say reaching out to touch his face one last time, to try to remember all the details but my hand just passed through. *'No!'* He screamed, trying to grasp my hand, *'Don't go!'*

My eyes were just starting to shut but I opened them and smiled at him. *'I'm just going to sleep; I will be alive when I wake up.'*

Now you're probably thinking, what happened? I do not understand

I don't know what happened and me neither. I guess you might if I explained it like how it is in my memories basically with terrible quality but stick with me.

It was the fourth of June. Pride Month! I know. Basically, the month that we closeted kids get very sad because we can't attend pride. And add that to the fact that there are no parades in Mumbai, and you have a lot of sadness, seeing pictures of people at the pride, smiling, laughing and being proud of themselves. Yeah, Pride Month for a closeted Indian kid hurts but we still love that there is a month for us.

I had met him a year and a day before at the bookstore while I was getting a copy of "The Seven Husbands of Evelyn Hugo", which everyone kept recommending. He was there alone too, looking for a book.

'What book are you looking for?' I asked because the store we were in, Book Lovers, didn't have that many variety so maybe it wasn't there.

'A very gay one.' Was his response. I had so many recommendations so before I could stop myself, I pointed out all of them in the store and how much I liked them, whether I had read them, if the TV adaptation of it was good or not.

God he was cute. No. Books. Talk about books. Wait, you've been talking for like fifty minutes. Stop talking. Shut Up. He will think you are crazy.

I shut my mouth right after talking about how I was excited for Volume 4 of Heartstopper. He was smiling and looking at me. Why was he smiling? I just proved to him what an idiot I am!

'My name's Noah.'

'I'm um- Taylor.'

'I like your name, Taylor.'

'Thanks.'

I'm pretty sure I was blushing so instead of going into further conversation which would probably lead to me embarrassing myself more, I turned to the shopkeeper. With very bad Hindi I asked him if the books I had asked him to order were there because I had the store send me a call if my book had come and arrived. It had. Where was the book? Right next to Noah. How could I get it? By asking Noah. What did asking Noah mean? Talking to him. What would happen if I talked to him? I'd put on my normal mask of confidence and ask him for it.

Zeus knew that was not going to happen, so I reached over to get it, the same time he turned, and I tripped and fell into him, scratching my arm on one of the shelves while trying to grab something to slow my fall. Blood was pouring out of the injury, and I realized that it was huge and deep and on my wrist.

That is great.

At the hospital on the bed, I couldn't get up and had to awkwardly raise my head as he tried to talk to me. On my bedside table, there was a copy of "The Seven Husbands Of Evelyn Hugo" and there was one in his hands too.

'I thought we could read this together.' He paused for a moment. *'If that's okay with you.'*

It very much was, so as I lifted it, gasping from the pain I opened page one, some words being covered by the gauze wrapped around my wrist.

'You are aware you're hurting yourself more by picking the book up?'

If pain was the cost to be able to read with him, then I would take it without hesitation.

He grabbed the book and set both down on my bedside table. *'We are going to read it when you can pick it up without hurting yourself.'*

We started talking a lot after I got out of the hospital. I got more and more confidence that he wouldn't hurt me, so I let myself be me. Authentic me who slept in classes because I slept at two and woke up at five. Me who had video calls with him at three while making pancakes, me who laughed during horror movies, who made terrible jokes about Wakanda forever in the intervals saying that the dude with wings on his feet had too much Red bull.

He didn't hate me for being non-binary and liking men, didn't tell me not to have a crush on him. Instead, he told me he was bisexual and that he knew what being closeted felt like.

When I came out to my family and my parents didn't accept me, he comforted me.

I think slowly I fell in love with him.

We were walking once (I know, finding a decent place to walk in Mumbai which isn't the beach was hard to find) when I tripped and almost fell face first into the gravel and glass, throwing up my arms to stop my fall. He made sure I was alright and then we saw what I tripped over. It was a book.

'*The secret of life.*' He read out loud.

Sounds nice, let's read it.

It contained some spells that probably didn't work so as a joke I tried one to see if I could become the fairy godmother in Cinderella, I said, '*bippity boppity boo*'. Nothing happened. Fair, that spell wasn't even in the book. I just wanted to try it.

I didn't try anything, it was obviously fake, why spend three minutes trying to recite a spell in a fiction book which looked like gibberish.

That night I turned up at Noah's house with a bag with everything I cared about, crying because I was finally kicked out by my family. He opened the door, smiling until he saw my tears. He rushed to me asking what happened.

His parents were looking in from their living room, trying to see who was at the door. He was closeted so I just turned around, trying to go but he stopped me. '*It's just my friend, they left something here.*' I had in fact left something there, I had left one of my hoodies because I had cold coffee spilled all over it, he had given me one of his hoodies which was way too large for me to go home in.

'*You have a friend?*'

'*Yes, Taylor, you know him.*' I knew he was using my birth pronouns because his parents were homophobic and if they found out either of us were queer, he'd be kicked out, but it made me a little sad. His parents still couldn't see us, so he mouthed '*Sorry*' to me. It was fine, I guess.

'Mom, can I have Taylor over for a sleepover?'

'Sure, just don't finish all the candies.'

'I don't know what you're talking about.'

'We aren't blind we see the bags of candy that you try to hide by putting them in your school bag.'

I smiled.

'I don't know what you're talking about.' he said with this confused and yet humorous tone of voice that he used to defend himself but also admit to being guilty.

He invited me in after I wiped my tears.

When we got into the room, he closed the door and sat me down on his bed, asking what happened. I just couldn't say it without crying but he got the gist.

'Your parents are assholes; you can stay here for some time.'

He didn't ask me to stop crying, he knew I needed to, instead he went and made a cold version of hot chocolate because he knew I liked it better cold, and gave it to me. Only when I held did I realize I was shaking. He waited for me to stop.

'You want to do something fun?' he asked, knowing I wasn't in the mood but just trying to lighten it, so I said, *'yes'*.

He took the book out, there was a spell that said it would take all the things that hurt away but if we messed it up there would be a major consequence. We flipped the page uninterested in getting our hopes up that we could get it right.

We could barely pronounce the words but once we figured it out, I tried out the spell for moving objects, I tried it on a pencil lying on his desk. Nothing happened. So, we tried all the weird spells in the book, trying to distract ourselves and then suddenly after an hour of doing stuff the pencil moved. That's weird there was nothing, no wind, no force to move it. I tried the spell again, this time pronouncing it right.

It turned over one side.

Noah and I both looked at each other with surprise and started laughing. He tried it, it barely moved but it still moved. No way!

Four days after that I was sleeping in Noah's bed right next to him, so close that if I reached out I could touch him but no. I can't. He does not like me that way. It had taken some time, but we were starting to get used to living in the same room, me in secret. He had a minifridge, so my food was always there, and his parents rarely checked the room so that was fine too. When he wasn't there, I would practice the spells, trying to pronounce them, trying to improve my understanding, trying to get ready to try the spell.

Time passed and one day I thought I was finally ready, he told me never to do it. He believed I could be cursed but what could be more of a curse than what was going on? So, one day when he left his room to go to school which was for some reason still on while my Diwali vacations were going on, I tried it. He walked back in, saying he forgot his pencil and he saw what I was doing.

And that was how I was gone. Because I messed up a spell which I had thought I had mastered. I cried and out of my body blood came in the place of tears. *'Taylor! You can't go!'* He was screaming and crying, and I wanted to comfort him, I wanted to hug him. I wanted to make his problems seem distant like they did for me when he was there.

'I cannot do this. I cannot.'

He picked up the book searching for something, something which he said would bring me back, but he found nothing.

When he could not find it, he threw the book.

'You can't leave me behind; I'm coming with you.' He started reciting the spell through his tears and that is when I started to fade, being dragged down by the anchor to the human world. It was working.

12

Voice Out the Voice In

by being_me_av

Its six hundred and a thirty rupees sir and here is your baggage. Please check, said Vinod; my cab driver. I paid him the fare and checked-in the hotel. The bell boy Shankar guided me to my room, placed my baggage in the storage area and asked me for any assistance I would like to have. As it was a long-haul travel, I had a cumbersome day and was totally exhausted and hungry. I had a quick look at the menu and asked to get me Pasta Pesto with a cream of mushroom hot soup. I was in the loo and heard my phone ringing. I came out and saw it was an unknown number, so I picked up and curiously asked, *'Hello Whos' This?'* The person on the other side greeted me good evening as it was dusk, and I greeted him too! He then said that he is Anand calling from Clingo Services and would like to confirm my appointment with Mr. Sam after two days as at present he is on a tour to Delhi. Mr. Sam was a Reiki Healer and a hypnotherapist. As I used to get anxious and impatient very quickly, so I thought to heal my situation from a professional expert. After hearing him out, I uttered that, coincidentally, I visited to Delhi for some project as well, so it will be great, that we fix up the appointment after two days. Anand, then confirmed me the appointment and hung up the call.

I was very nervous and feeling very uneasy as from the last few days things were quite tough for me to handle and was mostly unfavourable. I was seeking some sort of external push for me to internally buck up. Quite broke and tensed I sat on the upholstered chair and waited for my food to arrive.

I called Anand, to ask if Mr. Sam can see me in Delhi as both of us happened to be in there, to which Anand said that he needs to ask Mr. Sam about it and further asked me my location of stay. I shared that I was staying in Northern King Hotel, and he hung up the call. After five minutes I got a call, it was Anand and he said that it was a great coincidence that Mr. Sam have checked in at the same hotel as well. He further asked if I can see him in room no 211 in the next ten minutes, which was coincidentally the next room to mine. I was surprised, about these coincidences. I was also happy, that I was about to see him and was on the way to sort out my troubles which was very much required for me during these phases of my life. As scheduled, I went to his room and rang the doorbell. Hitesh his assistant, welcomed me in. It was a suite room; I went inside to see him.

Mr. Sam being a Reiki Healer and a hypnotherapist was a very spiritual person and was always in deep concentration and had deep power to read people and understand their situation. He saw me and said, why am I always anxious and tough with my life? What makes me feel that I will lose and what is the war that I am stuck with? What are my fears? I was a bit numb hearing him as I did not utter a word yet and he was very closely connecting with what I had to say. He looked into my eyes and said, *'Son what makes you the way you are and what are the struggles you think you are enduring?'* Then he asked me to share my problem. I felt a bit weird as well as it was precisely all my problems, I was about to ask him to which he already asked me to answer. I honestly didn't have any questions and was only left with his questions to be answered.

I started pondering about all that he queried from me. It puzzled me to a great extent because I visited him to get answers of these questions, hovering in my mind which were extremely uncomfortable. I looked answers to all of this, even have searched the internet but never got an authentic and true answer to any of this. After my friend Priyanka referred me about Mr. Sam and shared about him, I got a sigh of relief that to my goodness there exists an individual who can understand the conflicts and the dooms I have been going through. I was very much ferocious, very eager to see this personality and meet him in person to share my situation and get a solution. And after experiencing so many coincidences all at the same time, I finally happened to meet him in person, and, even before me uttering a single word he threw a set of questions onto me to answer which I precisely had to question him. I was awestricken! I was drifted, I requested Hitesh, his assistant, to get me a glass of water. After that, I was again lost in thoughts.

However, as Mr. Sam have questioned me, I was supposed to respond to him with each of his questions. I then said slowly that I don't know why I am facing such adversities and I actually don't want to be in such a phase. I said that I feel suffocated at times and overall is very disappointed and unhappy with my life. Many a times I feel nihilistic and helpless but must push with all the ongoing activities without a single percentage of my desire. I was just going with the flow and was sheer a strayed swaying here and there with no reason. I do not feel good and happy about all of it. Mr. Sam quietly listened to my rattles. His expression seemed that whatever I just said he already have asked me an answer to all. But still he very patiently listened to me and made me feel very comfortable. I was literally opening with all my problems and issues I was facing in my life in a quest internally to get a solution to all of it.

Then I was prompted my Mr. Sam to try to give an answer whatever according to me seemed to be an appropriate one to all his questions. I was comfortable in communicating to him and actually was feeling kind of relaxed and then I started answering to his set of questions.

I started with the first question; *'Why am I always anxious and tough with my life?'*

I said, I don't want to be tough but the ongoing circumstances in my life doesn't allow me to keep my calm and I become stern and worried.

Second question; *'What makes me feel that, I will lose, and what is the war that I am stuck with?'*

I said that I feel that if I don't stand up and rush to work I will be laid off and others will take my place, so I compare my results and bandwidth with others and try to win over them.

Third question; *'What are my fears?'*

I said I fear to be left behind and aloof.

Fourth question; *'What makes you the way you are and what are the struggles you think you are enduring?'*

I said, I have become like this because of the external pushes I receive on a daily basis through various people, and I don't want to fail to match up to their opinions and I struggle to keep up with all their opinions . These things keep me worried, and I feel greatly adverse. These things keep me bothered and stiff.

I sip over the remaining water in the glass as I was done and remained silent now.

Mr. Sam was gazing at me immensely. It looked like he understood, my conflicts, and now had an answer to all of it. I was quite eager to listen to his point of view and quite impatient internally to get a one-shot solution to all of it.

He then exclaimed again with a question and asked; *'In all this process what have you actually lost?'*

I was shaken as it was time for me to reveal that I have lost my own self, my peace and my individuality. I said all this to him.

Hearing to which made him ask me, *'On whose command did I do so?'* He further asked, *'Was there anybody who forced me or have threatened me to act the way I had acted all this time?'*

I was very sure on this, and I instantly said a no that there wasn't anyone under whose influence I was compelled to act in this way.

He said why did you become like this then if no one made you do this neither you've learned to do it from anyone. He continued that by and large each attribute of mine have been formed inside my mind. Each of my anxiousness, fear, struggles, toughness etc. are formed from my own mind. I am having a war with my own self, all the conflicts which I think prevails over me from external forces are with my inner self. I quietly listened to him and was realizing that he was certainly right.

Ting Tong…Ting Tong! The doorbell rang continuously. I stood up and opened the door; it was Shankar the bell boy. He has come with my food order; I was petrified as I was in the next room, and he got me the order there without me asking him. I however asked him to keep the food on the table, signed the invoice and he took a leave. I did not question him anything as I had to continue my communication with Mr. Sam. I went to the loo to sprinkle water on my face as I was feeling drowsy and after I came out there was no one in the room. I could only find my luggage stored, the food kept on the table and myself stood up amazed. I was very petrified now and deeply confounded. I went out of my room and checked around, there was no sight of room no 211. I immediately called up the reception and asked about the guest staying in room no 211 and her response shook me up. She said, *'Sir there is no room no 211 in our entire hotel. In second floor we have rooms from 201 to 210 and on the third floor its continued from 301 to 310. All room numbers are allotted in each floor in this sequence.'* I hung up the phone, had a glass of water and sat down again. I checked my phone and to my utter surprise I never received any call from an unknown number after I checked in the hotel and the last call on my log was the contact number of Vinod, the cab driver. Was it all a dream? I enquired myself!

I was feeling very uneasy, and I gave a call to my friend Priyanka and enquired from her about Mr. Sam. She started laughing on my enquiry as she told me that she never referred me to any Mr. Sam and was quite hypothetical whether he exists also or not. I greeted her bye and hung the phone. Lately but I realized now that all this was a dream I saw in the interim after Shankar the bell boy left taking my food order and the time he got it delivered to me. I remembered that I sat down on the upholstered sofa after he took my order and as I was tired, I might have taken a deep nap in the interim. But in this short couple of minutes, I was taught a great life lesson and applied logic about who gave it to me? I was struggling with all the issues I have mentioned in my dream and was seeking solution to it. Was it my inner voice, God or some pure spirit who came and taught me this. Whosoever it was, I certainly got answers to all of it and without applying any external effort got authentic solutions to it. I felt light and better and there was a broad smile on my face. I felt soothe and calm from inside and I started enjoying the hot meal been delivered by Shankar.

I was really startled by it and realized something within me started transforming. I simply was enjoying the process and was deeply happy from inside. Days passed, I was involved with my chores, met people, and got along with my life as normal. But there was a new me, a new personality all over who really did not bother about others' opinions neither was afraid about anything and just did things which gave me peace and made me happy internally. For few days I was mocked by people seeing an absolute new version of myself but gradually they got acquainted to me and surprisingly I received more love, honour, and respect from everyone who liked me being my own self and living an authentic, fearless, purposeful life.

Frankly I did not apply much logic to what happened in that dream of mine and only focused on the good outcomes came out of it. I still believed before that golden hour, there was a story and impression that I had formed about myself over my mind and all of that multiplied and hovered over me every single day. Same thing majority of us does unconsciously. But there is one more world than the external world in which we live in and that's our internal world. We live many lives there; sometimes negative, sometimes positive. It's up to our own perception which life we want to live from so many lives we have formed for us in our own little internal world. So why don't we get liberated from all sorts of flaws and negativities and embrace positivity into our lives and live a genuine, pure, and authentic life happily and peacefully. This internal voice of God or whatever it was shook me up, from a low level to an absolute level and changed my overall perception about life. Today I breath very happily and peacefully and all that happened only after that golden hour in that hotel.

12

Lauren

by Sandhita Agarwal

Lauren sighed into her phone. It had been a while since she last saw Matt. She missed their date nights. She missed junk food. She had been cooking at home since the lockdown. She was so bored. She browsed through the movies on Netflix. Everything seemed stale like a hot, dry day in the desert. Her family and she had been to the sand dunes in India last year. Though she had loved staying in the tents and the camel rides, she had always felt sick to her stomach because of the hot, dry air. She started watching videos on You-tube. She got bored soon. She wanted to play a game. She went to the apple store hoping to find an interesting game. An app caught her eye. *'Playlist, Get naughty with playlists.'* She downloaded the app. The app opened with a single question on the screen. How many items do you want to add to your playlist? Without thinking she typed in 100. A progress bar popped up. A few seconds later, a card popped up with a guy's details. Damn! It was just another dating app. Instead of a green tick, the card had a cross and a text field for a number. Maybe she had to score the guy. The guy was cute. She gave him a 9 and pressed next. A toast popped up saying *'Item added to list.'* What the hell! She thought. What sort of a list was this? The next guy popped up soon after. He was an older guy with a moustache, a no-no! She pressed the cross. *'Item rejected.'* Suddenly, Jim from work popped up on the app. Lauren felt her throat tighten. She did not want guys from work to find out that she was on a dating app. She tried closing the app. But there was no exit button. That was annoying. She pressed everywhere. The app wouldn't close. *'Stupid, horribly designed app.'* She restarted her phone. Nothing worked. She went online and searched, but Nothing. She went to the apple store to look up the developer information. It was developed by a company named "Crystal Labs." There was no contact info. She googled, no luck. She was getting frustrated. She went back to the app and started rejecting everyone. After rejecting 10 guys, a warning popped up *'You cannot reject more than 10 items in one day.'* She threw the phone onto her bed and went for a shower. The water felt cool and relaxing. After the much-needed shower, she fixed herself a roast beef sandwich and sat down to her meal. Her mind was working better now. She wanted to reach out to her friend and ask him about the app. But this was too embarrassing. There was no logical explanation as to why she had downloaded a weird app, especially when the app advertised a naughty playlist. There was only one way to go and that was forward. She should get to the end and maybe then the exit button would be visible. She quickly finished her sandwich and picked up her phone. She had scored another five guys and was confused. She had scored everyone from 1 to 10. Another profile popped up. It was her crush from her office. Her heart skipped a beat. What the hell! She sceptically typed in 10 and pressed next. The app rejected the score with a pop-up that said, *'Position already filled.'* She was getting a sinking feeling in her stomach. She tried typing in 8 but still the same message. She then types in 11 and a new profile popped up. *'Ah. So, I am basically sorting these guys into a list. But what for?'* Her anxiety rose a notch. Another 20 minutes passed by. Lauren couldn't believe she was nearing 100! She scored the last guy with a 100. The app started vibrating as soon as she clicked next. Her stomach started sinking. And for no apparent reason, a chill ran down her spine. A playlist opened on the app. The first item in the playlist was a guy called Rob. Lauren couldn't believe what she was seeing on the phone. The playlist made no sense. At least the exit button was visible now. She quickly exited the app and saw that she had 2 missed calls. The first one is from Matt and the second from an unknown number. She called up Matt and related the whole incident to him. As expected, Matt was pissed with her. He couldn't provide any insights but offered to drop in for the night. She was grateful for that. The app had completely creeped her out. Lauren wandered into the kitchen to cook something for Matt. Her cell phone rang. The same unknown number. Instinct told Lauren not to answer the call. She poured herself a glass of wine and started cooking butter chicken. Soon the kitchen was permeated with the aromas of curry and naan. The doorbell rang as she was finishing up in the kitchen. Lauren straightened her dress and moved to open the door. It wasn't Matt at the door. It was a stranger. He introduced himself as Rob. Lauren suddenly realized who this was. The stranger from the app. She felt sick to her stomach and quickly closed the door. The damn app had sent requests to all the guys!! What was she supposed to do now? The guy on the other side of the door kept pleading for her to open the door. She took a deep breath and asked him what he wanted. He told her he loved her and wanted to be with her. Lauren started to panic. She knew she had to stay calm. Nothing had happened and she was in control. She got her phone from the kitchen and dialled Matt. Matt was on his way, just a few minutes away. With her heart pounding in her chest, she went to look through the peephole. The guy was just standing there, staring at the door. She saw Matt jumping out of his car, running towards the man. The man turned around and with a sudden animalistic growl jumped on Matt. There was a moment of shock on Matt's face before he went down. The man bit his neck and pulled out a huge chunk of flesh. Lauren screamed and moved to open the door. She stopped and quickly dialled 911. The dispatcher told her to stay inside the house. She hung up and screamed at the man. The man stopped, his expression changing. He started apologizing and moving towards the door. First, there was pleading, then the man started banging his fists on the door. Lauren couldn't understand what was happening. Matt was gurgling and seemed to be fading fast. The door was starting to crack from the blows. Lauren ran into the kitchen and grabbed her biggest knife. She moved away from the door with the knife pointed in her hand. The door was going to break, and she was going to die. Matt was going to die and all because she downloaded some stupid app. She suddenly broke out of her self-pity and ran into her bedroom. She went into her bathroom and locked the door. She pushed her dressing table against the door and waited. There was a loud bang outside. The door had given away. He was in the house now. *'Lauren!'* A sweet sickly voice called out. *'Come out honey. I love you. I just want to be with you.'* She swallowed the sobs forming in her throat. She wanted to do a lot of things in life. This was not how she wanted to go, killed by a psychopath because of some shitty app. The man stopped outside the door. *'Lauren, I know you're in there. I can feel you'* Lauren couldn't believe it. Was he some supernatural entity? A zombie-vampire-werewolf with superhuman strength and tracking skills? She couldn't fight something like that. Lauren started hyperventilating. The man was pounding into the door now, wood splintering and hinges cracking. Lauren felt her life coming to an end. And yet she refused to die again. She opened the closet under the sink and picked up the bottle of bleach. She was going to throw the bleach at him and then stab him. She had to try. As she prepared for the attack, sirens wailed in the distance. The police were coming? Was she going to be saved? The man suddenly stopped. He backed away into the room and Lauren heard him running away. She decided to wait for the police. She soon heard voices coming from the front door. She called out to the police. She was still afraid to open the bathroom door. A female voice was asking her to open the door. Lauren slowly opened the door. Lauren ran to the front of the house. The paramedics were trying to revive Matt. Lauren woke up in a white room. Everything was white and harsh in her eyes. Her mind tried to grasp at the memories that seemed to flit in and out. She saw someone dressed in white approach her. *'Lauren!' 'Can you hear me?'* The fog was slowly lifting from her thoughts and one face cut through the mistiness of the moment. *'Where is Matt?'* The woman in white pursed her lips, turned around, and left the room. This shocked Lauren into lucidity. Something had happened to Matt. As Lauren was trying to get up, a doctor entered the room. *'Hey take it easy. Matt's fine'* She didn't believe him. She demanded that she be taken to see Matt. The doctor looked at her pensively for a moment before leading her into the corridor. On the way to the ICU, the doctor explained that she had hit her head on the ground when she passed out and was being treated for a mild concussion. Matt had lost a lot of blood but had pulled through. Tears rolled down her cheeks when she realized how close she had come to losing him. The doctor led her back to her room where lunch was waiting for her. She was famished. The nurse woke her up for her medicines. She popped the pills into her mouth and drank from the tiny water cup. The nurse informed her that she would be under observation for the night and would probably be discharged the next day. Matt however was going to take longer to convalesce. The nurse came in and introduced Lauren to Detective Rogers. The detective interviewed her, and she told him everything about the app. Lauren could see that the detective found it hard to believe her. She started searching for the app on her phone to prove them. She couldn't find it. The detective asked her a few more questions about Rob's appearance and assured her that they would try to catch him soon. Lauren knew something weird was happening. The news flash caught her attention. A body was found in a ditch near her home and the man's driving license identified him as Rob Lowey. The man was found naked with bite marks all over his body. Lauren couldn't believe that this story would get more complicated like this. Her only fear was that if Matt had been bitten by a werewolf or a vampire or some supernatural being, he was going to turn too. She woke up in the morning to a ping on her phone. She looked at the screen. Playlist: Item 2 is now playing. Her jaw dropped and she quickly tapped on the notification. The Playlist app opened with the creepy, moustached man as the next item playing. Lauren started sobbing. She had had enough of this. She tried uninstalling the app. This was something beyond her understanding. Someone had hacked into her phone and was now doing this. But who and why? Lauren was discharged in the noon and was on her way home in an Uber. Matt was still in the hospital. Her heart was pounding as she walked to her door. No moustached man was hanging around. She breathed a sigh of relief and entered her home. The doors had been repaired and reinforced as she had requested. As evening rolled around, Lauren started feeling queasy. She pushed her sofa up against the door and walked around the house making sure every window was closed. She then poured herself a glass of wine. She prayed for Matt's speedy recovery. It was when she was finishing her sixth glass, that she heard it. Someone was at her door. She slowly moved aside the curtain and peeked out the window. It was the moustached guy. He was mumbling something to himself and staring at the door. She backed away from the door and holed herself in the bathroom. She dialled 911 and told the dispatcher what happened. The police took the moustached man into custody. Lauren went online to see if she could find any answers, but nothing. It was truly bizarre. She transferred her sim to her spare android phone. She switched the phone on and saw the playlist app. It was like getting stuck in one of those psychological thrillers where the events happened in a loop. The next morning Lauren was at the police station at the detective's request. The man in custody was called Michael Jacobs. The man was catatonic, and they could extract no information from him. Lauren was questioned by the detective about her involvement with Michael. She told him about the app again and that she had never seen him before. She whipped out her phone to show him the screenshots. Just as she had feared, there were no such screenshots in her gallery or on the cloud. And no app on her phone. She started crying. The detective tried soothing her and promised police protection for the next few days. Her phone started ringing. The detective urged her to pick up. It was Matt's doctor. He wanted her to come down to the hospital as Matt was requesting to see her. She felt a bit weird that the doctor had called and not the hospital admin. Matt looked better, and he smiled at her. They chatted happily for a while. The doctor came in and told her that she was welcome to spend the night at the hospital and they could both leave early the next day. Lauren was confused and didn't have any of her stuff with her for the night. But the doctor was insistent. She worried that it was something related to Matt's health, and she agreed. As the night rolled in, she got a call from the detective on her phone. The detective told her that the bites and wounds on Rob's body were self-inflicted. All evidence seemed to point to a suicide. Before disconnecting the call, the detective also told her that Michael Jacobs had been transferred to a psychiatric ward since he had tried to scoop out his own eyes with a spoon. Lauren was shocked. What was wrong with these guys? She felt sick. She relayed the information to Matt. He understood how she felt. They hugged each other for some time. Lauren lay down on the sofa next to Matt's bed and fell asleep. She dreamt about a long corridor with endless doors. As she opened the first door, Rob jumped out at her. She quickly closed the door and moved to the next door. As expected, it was Michael with a menacing look in his eyes. She shut the door and moved to the next one. She slowly opened the door and saw him. And she screamed. Her own scream woke her up. She woke up to darkness. For a moment she felt intense panic and disorientation. But then slowly her mind brought back memories of the day and her breathing slowed down. He eyes soon adjusted to the darkness and she saw Matt sleeping in his bed. The clock read 1:30 am. She got up to use the restroom. When she returned, she saw a silhouette sitting on the sofa she had been sleeping on. Her heart jumped to her chest. She rushed to Matt and tried to wake him up. *'He won't be waking up so soon.'* The voice said and she recognized that voice. It was the doctor. Before she could say or do anything the doctor ran to her, pinned one arm behind her back with one hand and the other across her mouth effectively silencing her. He started dragging her to the corridor. As soon as they were in the hallway, Lauren kicked the man's shins with all her might. The doctor buckled over in pain releasing her. She then jammed her elbow into his neck and ran towards the exit. She took the stairs 3 at a time to the parking. It was only when she had got into her car that she calmed down a bit. Had the doctor killed Matt? Tears welled up in her eyes. Matt was suffering too much because of her. She knew why the doctor was behaving that way. She fished out her phone from her pocket. At the top, it was the Playlist list app. When she opened it, she saw the doctor's face stare up at her. Lauren quickly called up the detective. A groggy voice picked up after a few rings. She filled him on what was happening. The detective agreed to meet her at her home. She and the detective were soon sitting in her living room. The detective was looking at the playlist app on Lauren's phone, his eyebrows bunched together. *'How come you do not remember numbering the doctor?' 'That's the thing Detective. I cannot remember any of these faces popping up on the app. I will surely have remembered.'* Lauren replied. *'By the way, I forgot to tell you, Michael is on suicide watch. He tried to kill himself again.' 'Oh!'* They both sat there confused. *'I am just scared about what these men are trying to do to me. Are they trying to kill me? And if they are unsuccessful, they kill themselves? Or more complicated? A list item destroying itself to make space for more list items on the screen?'* Lauren pondered aloud. *'I don't know what to say, Lauren. I have never seen anything like this before. You said there were 100 items on the list. I shudder to think what that means. We need to know more.'* Lauren cut him off. *'I know what you want me to do. We need to know what these men want from me. But I am scared Detective.' 'I will be there at every step Lauren. I just want to know what we are up against and find ways to handle and resolve this situation. Meanwhile, I have called in our IT guys. They will be cloning your phone and looking for ways to hack into the app. There is a guard stationed in Matt's room and he will be safe there. You and I should work on the plan now. Does this sound ok to you?'* Lauren nodded. They spent the next hour coming up with a plan. She dialled the doctor's number. *'Hi. Dr. Maloney. I am sorry about the way I left things. I just wasn't feeling well.' 'Oh, Lauren. I am so happy you called. I was going crazy. I just feel so incomplete without you. I just don't feel like breathing without you next to me.'* Replied Dr. Maloney. Lauren bit her lips and said, *'Why don't you come over doctor? Let's get better acquainted.' 'I'll be right there!'* With the detective hiding in the guest bedroom, Lauren felt a bit relieved. She was still very nervous. Just follow the plan. She thought in her head. They needed to know more. Just then her doorbell rang. She walked to the door and there stood the doctor in a black suit and tie. He had a bottle of champagne in his hand, and he was smiling warmly. Lauren invited him inside. She sat down next to him. He was funny and warm. Soon they were talking animatedly about horror movies and Lauren forgot all about the app. The champagne was excellent, and he had ordered take-out from Lauren's favourite Mexican restaurant. How had he known? It seemed like Dr Maloney already knew a lot about Lauren. She finally asked the doctor how he knew so much about her. The doctor's answer shocked Lauren. *'Yesterday as soon as the clock struck 12, I just fell in love with you. And I have spent hours scouring the internet looking up information on you. I don't mean to sound like a stalker, but I love everything about you. Your beautiful brown eyes. Your long black hair. The way your eyes crinkle up when you smile. I know you are a kind, generous person. I feel like you're exactly the woman I was waiting for my whole life.'* The conviction with which the doctor said these words made Lauren blush. What if he was in love with her for real? What if the app was helping her choose her soulmate? Her mind started buzzing with confusing questions and foreign emotions. The bell rang again. Their food had arrived. As they both sat down to a delicious meal, Lauren realized she hadn't had this much fun in a very long time. Her relationship with Matt had become robotic. They hardly talked anymore. She looked up to see the doctor staring at her. *'You look so beautiful and innocent just sitting there. I feel so blessed that I am having this amazing meal with you and it's one of the very few perfect moments in my life.'* The doctor commented. Lauren blushed deeply. And to her amazement, she could feel her need in her loins. As the doctor leaned in for a kiss, Lauren responded passionately. Soon they were naked in each other's arms, panting and moaning with the twin needs of their bodies. And soon Lauren felt a huge explosion inside of her and she was flying over a vast, white ocean. She lay in his arms, spent and happy. She must have fallen asleep because she awoke to the doctor getting dressed. Her clock read 12:06 am. 'Are you leaving?' Lauren muttered; her head groggy. *'Err. I am sorry Lauren. I don't know what happened to me. I guess I was just lost in the heat of the moment. You are a wonderful woman, and any guy would be lucky to have you. I just don't think this is going to work out in the long run.'* The doctor apologized. He picked up his wallet and before Lauren could respond, dashed out of the bedroom, opened the front door, and disappeared into the night. Lauren lay in bed stunned. Her eyes were beginning to sting with the threat of tears when the detective walked into the room. Lauren quickly pulled the sheets up around her. She had completely forgotten about the detective. *'I think I know what's happening here, Lauren.'* The detective said. *'The app lines up dates for you and if they don't have sex with you, they commit suicide. But if they sleep with you, they are done with you.'* Lauren felt humiliated and sad. This was like her college dating scene all over again. The detective was going on and on and preaching to her like the pastor at her church. Lauren felt like slapping him. *'You made me do it.'* Lauren interjected the detective. *'I didn't even want to see the guy again. You said you wanted to see what happens and go with the flow and now you're judging me. Get out of my house.'* Lauren screamed. The detective stood there with his mouth half-open. *'I am sorry. Yes, I made you do it. I take everything back.'* Lauren softened a bit at that but couldn't help noticing the sneer on the detective's face. Once Lauren was fully clothed, they started discussing the next steps. *'I got a call from my tech team and it's impossible to hack the app. It's not a normal app Lauren. It doesn't have any online presence. Tech team was unable to figure out how you even downloaded the app.'* The detective said morosely. *'There are some larger forces at play here. I can't believe I am saying this but there's something supernatural about the app.'* Then, Lauren asked through the sobs about what she's gonna do. *'I can't sleep with these men. I feel like killing myself and ending this nightmare.'* Lauren wailed. The detective was about to say something when there was a loud knock at the door. Lauren started shaking violently. *'No. don't let him come in.'* The detective peeped out through the peephole and saw a handsome man standing on the doorstep with a bouquet of roses in his hands. The man looked at the peephole and smiled. The detective felt a shiver run down his spine. Lauren was a complete mess, and every sound made her jump violently. Just then her phone rang. It was Matt. She told Matt everything that had happened till now. To her immense relief, Matt was supportive and consoling. She realized how foolish she had been. She had been ready to give up their relationship for a few moments of excitement. She was no better than the men the app had lined up for her. Those men were at least under some supernatural influence. What excuse did she have? She was about to say something when the detective motioned her to disconnect the call. She apologized to Matt and hung up. *'I may have some good news!'* Lauren's heart began to fill up with hope. *'The tech team has found a clause in the privacy agreement. If you get married, then the playlist gets dissolved.'* The detective said casually. *'What? If I get married, that's it?' 'Apparently, yes.'* The detective clarified. She dialed Matt's number and explained the option to him. There was a silence at the other end. *'Err Lauren. You know I love you, but I am not sure I am ready for marriage at this point.'* Matt replied. Lauren's heart sank when she heard his response. *'But we can just get married till the playlist dissolves and if you really don't want to stay married, we can end the marriage.'* Lauren implored. *'I don't think that's how things work Lauren. I am sorry I can't do this.'* With that Matt disconnected the call. Lauren had never expected Matt to behave like this. Had she taken him for granted all this time? The straw of hope that Lauren had been clutching onto started slipping away from her. The detective finally spoke. *'I'll marry you. I know we barely know each other but I want to help you. We can end the marriage once you are out of this mess.'* Lauren had never properly seen him until now. He had just been the kind police guy helping her. But now she saw his kind eyes, his gentle mouth, and his broad shoulders. It was weird how quickly her perspective shifted. She had a new respect for this man. The wedding arrangements were made at a local pizzeria. Lauren was dressed in a simple white cocktail gown. Her eyes were still red from the copious amounts of tears she had shed in the past 4 hours. It was 5 am. They stealthily made their way out of the house. The detective had a smart black suit on. He looked dashing. He had his gun drawn out just in case. As they slowly made out the door, a figure was lying prone on the lawn outside. It jumped up as soon it saw them. It was the man from before. Lauren hid behind the detective as the detective warned the man not to approach them. The man seemed to listen to them as he stood still. Lauren and the detective quickly got into the detective's car and started backing out of the driveway. Suddenly the man jumped onto the car's bonnet and started licking the windscreen. The detective pressed the brakes, and the man was thrown off. The detective quickly backed out and sped away. At the run-down pizzeria called Gustave's pizza, Lauren was standing next to the detective and completing the final oaths. *'Yes, I do.'* As soon as the wedding was done, Lauren pulled her phone out and looked at the notification on the top. The notification that had made her heart sink to the bottom of her stomach every time she had looked at it. The notification now had a cancellation in front of the man's face. The list number, which was earlier 4, was now blank, it disappeared completely, and the app closed on its own. She felt immense relief rush through her body, and she fell. The detective caught her as her knees buckled under her. *'Is it gone?'* He asked. She nodded and hugged him tightly. The nightmare was over. I would like to say that all of them learned something from this ordeal except of course the people who died. RIP. Lauren learned not to download strange apps. She also learned a few things about love and relationships. Because you see they didn't end the marriage after all. They discovered that sharing such a strange ordeal had bonded them in a way that they could never be separated again. And for this once they did live happily ever after.

14

Guy From Zorath

by Hyder Khan

AI said, *'Landing successful planet seems to have breathable environment.'*

Guy: *Analyze atmospheric composition. What is that sound? Analyze!*

AI: *Sound incoming from northwest 20 meters ahead, analyzing further.*

Guy: *Activate universal translation function.*

Gen: *You will now pay for your crimes against the Giga empire Saito.*

I am going to whip your skin off, remember who your lords are.

Saito: *General we will never serve you till one of us live, the people of Feze will rebel against your tyranny.*

Guy's eyes turned red, he said enough! And blasted a high intensity laser through his eyes and burned the general's head in one shot. Soldiers immediately charged towards him and were ripped to shreds as he tore them limb from limb with his bare hands, blood sprayed all over Saito's face. The remaining soldiers began to run to their ships in fear of their lives after what they had witnessed. Saito regained composure, jumped, and picked up a gun and killed a few of them trying to escape and turned around to see Guy 15 feet above the ground eviscerating dozens of them by blasting them from his laser vision.

Guy started walking towards his ship, '*prepare exit, this is some kind of mud show*' he said.

Saito pleaded '*stop great warrior! I am Saito king of the Feze race, please help us*'.

I have never witnessed powers and strength as great as yours, the warring factions of Alpha and Delta are hell bent on taking over this planet in their battle for mineral nefra which powers their high-tech weapons.

Guy introduced himself and asked Saito to continue.

It all started 10 years ago our planet was surrounded by a deadly pandemic, thousands of people were dying every day, my daughter Huna had also fallen ill, and we had all lost hope.

That night there was a light filling up the night sky of our Capital, it was them. Thousands of celestial ships surrounding a large ship hovering right above the palace, it was a sight we had never seen. Our religious scriptures had spoken of such ships, which our ancestors had arrived in to begin life on this planet eons ago.

There was panic on the streets as everyone thought the Gods themselves have descended to end us and finish all life as we know it. Then they arrived, thousands of them in shining silver armours with the empires crest, they revealed their faces which showed they were life forms just like us. Their messenger informed us he was sent by emperor Arafio of the great empire of planet Gigatron and they had come in peace to learn more about life on other planets and that is how they found our planet. He then told us the emperor himself will arrive any moment to visit us.

Suddenly sounds of drums beating could be heard, the sounds grew louder and behold the emperor himself came beaming through the ship, dressed in a shining Golden armour.

'Greetings oh king of Feze!' he said, and firmly shook my hand, then gestured towards the door his army entered with crates of gifts of all kinds and there were animal life forms we had never seen. Then I informed him of the grave pandemic that had plagued our planet, he ordered his scientists to analyze it. Within few days they came back and gifted our planet the greatest thing we could possibly hope for, it was the antidote for the plague!

This was the start of a great relation between our planet and the Giga empire. They gave us the antidote and advanced technology in exchange for the rare mineral nefra on our planet. All was peaceful until their emperor was alive and one dreadful day he was poisoned. Nobody knew how it happened but as soon as he died, his two sons Aretho and Bravo started fighting for the control of the empire and a civil war broke out amongst the two heirs of the once peaceful empire.

The emperor had ordered his son Bravo to replace him in such an event, however Aretho was not happy and accused his brother of poisoning the emperor. In a bid to control the empire Aretho occupied our planet, I had to escape and have been hiding for years, please help us.

Guy said, *'where's this Bravo then?'*

He moved his armies to planet Hersa and has been launching multiple conquests on our planet against Aretho's viceroy and son Kravat. Battles were fought everywhere on our planet and in space. Millions have died in the civil war on both sides.

(Kravat is a dreadful demon who can breathe fire, on his arrival he burned down thousands of my subjects and massacred them.)

People ran as his armies invaded the planet and painted the streets red with the blood of my subjects, he showed no mercy and forcefully enslaved our population to mine the nefra. He destroyed our religious relics and burned down our temples and forced my subjects to pledge allegiance to the empire, he declared his father Aretho to be our God the only one and worthy of devotion and praise. Life as we know was destroyed all in the name of the empire, millions killed and separated from their families.

When my family tried to escape, he captured them, thousands of people gathered on the palace grounds to beg for mercy, but he burned them alive on the palace grounds for them to witness. I could only watch in agony from a distance as it happened before my own eyes. I have been in hiding for years since then only to see my planet go further in flames and my subjects being enslaved. I have been trying to regroup my army but there was no hope.

A priest then informed me he knew a way of finding "Veritas", a secret weapon hidden by our ancestors long ago to protect the planet, also mentioned in our scriptures. I began an expedition to recover it, believed to be hidden somewhere in the jungles of dibo, a weapon powerful enough to destroy a planet!

After 6 months of excavations, we found it. There it was deep within the forest in underground caves, we then found the device which appeared like a cylinder, and it required a key. The key was this royal family crest locket, I am wearing right now passed on through generations.

When I inserted the key, the device was activated, and asked me, what was "Veritas" I replied it is a weapon created by our ancestors, to which the device replied, 'you do not know Veritas' and released a blinding beacon laser into the sky and disappeared right in front of our eyes.

Guy interrupted, so that was what my systems detected!

I travel across the cosmos looking for life forms and artifacts and my systems indicated intelligent life on this planet. I have heard of Veritas before on another planet, but they had a different name for its "Genesis" but a very similar story. However, the natives of planet

Sozos have been looking for centuries and have not come across it.

Saito said, '*how is this possible, where is this planet?*'.

Guy replied, '*It is possible we all look the same, the few lives form I have encountered. Although only your planet and Sozos who are 2 light years away have mentioned Veritas. We on my planet Zorath have discovered hyper space travel, we still do not have a weapon that can level a planet like you mentioned.*'

Saito inquired further, '*wait few, how many life forms have you encountered? what do you mean we all look the same?*'

Guy explained. '*So far including yours and the empire, we all look the same physically. The empire is the only planetary civilization I have seen in 20 years who have some military and scientific capability comparable to us. The origins of life on our planet Zorath are a mystery as well, it is believed all records containing the information were destroyed several millennia ago when we had our own great civil war. I will help you, maybe we can uncover more but first let us teach the empire a lesson.*'

Guy asked, '*where do I find Kravat?*'

Saito said, '*he is in my palace, here on this map.*'

Before Saito could inquire further, Guy blasted off vertically up to the upper ends of the planet's atmosphere and straight bombed himself through the forcefield protecting the palace, the impact created a shockwave through the city, shattering glass and blowing debris across a 3km radius. The army started receding from the borders of the capital toward the palace, all alarms went off around the capital.

There was Guy right in the palace grounds, special guards started to surround him. Guy flew past them and broke into the court, destroying gate after gate before anyone could react grabbed Kravat by the hair and flung him at the giant idol of his father.

After a moment everyone present in the room realized what they witnessed, took their laser guns out and started shooting at Guy, who retaliated by eviscerating each one of them with his laser vision. He then saw the guards near the grounds were approaching the court he picked up the statue's giant head and threw it at them squashing hundreds like a cannon ball, spraying the walls in red.

Guy turned around and dodged Kravat's fire breath which burned the chairs present in the court, creating a huge fire. Guy then hit Kravat with a laser vision blast who retaliated by his fire breath the paths of the blasts collided, both tried to burn the other down but Kravat overpowered Guy and knocked him through the wall into the palace grounds. Then he charged towards Guy and hit him with a powerful punch knocking him through the boundary walls of the first compound.

Guy charged back flying with full force towards Kravat, who replied by another fire blast, Guy dodged the blast choked Kravat by the neck and flew him higher and high into space before Kravat could react with another fire blast, they were in space where Kravat couldn't breathe. Guy then crushed Kravat's windpipe and pulled it right out of his throat and knocked his head off his body with a hand chop! Guy grabbed Kravat's body by the leg in one hand and grabbed the head by the other and flew back down to the palace and threw the body near the palace gates and flew off with the head.

Mutiny broke out as the natives started attacking the soldiers and snatching their weapons and overpowering them, after what they had seen.

Saito arrived near the palace amidst the whole chaos and was trying to get close, people were fighting all around. Guy landed right in front of him with Kravat's head bringing the whole stampede to a halt. The crowds were shocked, and, Guy said, *'You have 10 minutes, if I see a single silver armour present here. I swear on the Giga empire, you will meet the same fate as your master.'*

Millions across the planet witnessed in celebration as thousands of spaceships evacuated the planet and the army of the empire retreated. Saito thanked Guy and wished him good fortune and success. Guy took off in his ship and looked at his next destination.

AI: *Destination confirmed, tracking radiation trail to planet Hersa.*

Guy: *Good! I want to gift Kravat's head to Bravo. Maybe that fool will lead us to Veritas.*

15

The Machine Made

by Mukul Namagiri

PAGE 1 PLAYERS; CHARACTER TRAITS PROTAGONIST referred as PT YOUND LAD (TROUBLED, DEEP PAIN, SORDID PAST, HIDING PAIN, UNEASE, PARANOID) WORKER referred as boy (PALE, MUTE, SUNKEN EYES, SIGNS OF HARD LABOUR) ANTAGONIST referred as AT THE WISER (PRAGMATIC, RUSTY LOOKING, GRUMPY OLD MAN, ABUSIVE, DELUSIONAL)

PAGE 2 SETTING; RUSTY OLD INDUSTRIAL FACTORY WITH HEAVY METAL WORKS

PAGE 3 Exterior: factory dawn SCENE DESCRIPTION: The silhouette of a bleak stone BUILDING, no bigger than an Acre PILOT ROCK. A few ramshackle outbuildings cling to the surface like barnacles. On the highest point of the FACTORY stands a tall, crumbling. CHIMNEY Black smoke puffs from its crooked chimney. The third-rate engine rumbles creating a sense of unease for all the people for there were none. It is a small place with no living breathing soul for miles nothing but abandoned factories and thick dense forests till the miles end.

Character description: One man is YOUNG (early 20s). Tall, athletic -- but starved. His deep-set eyes are haunted, and his left eye is healing from a week-old shiner. His crooked expression is severe. There is an eerie disquiet about him. A small moustache shows his vanity. The other is OLD. His weathered, feral bearded, and hunched, with hands like vices. His lack of visible lips suggests some missing teeth. He tremors a bit, but he is lean and sturdy as a lead pipe. His high cheekbones smile even when he grimaces. His wild eyes shine like jewels. He is an old Pan. Monologue (read in the voice of the narrator)

PT: (rambling) when ye be in the slumbering in deep slumber me the worker be sweating the mid night oil to keep them machines running. I barley closed my eyes for it has been 2 days. The maftin near the machines makes you go crazy. The constant noises from the miller. I went past the Oldman's quarters he was in his deepest slumber. I could not with stand his snoring I had a fit of rage. The only thing stopping me from bashing his brains out is the severance pay he has been holding. Oo, I dreamt about its night after night by never have I ever touched the old soul. Interior: lunch break night.

SCENE DESCRIPTION: The two men sit in the cramped galley. A kerosene lamp flickers on the table between them, they show a sigh of comfort after the exhaustion at the factory

AT: To the fine days here, my, lad! (Raising his hand and passing a cup of thick liquid, most probably some kind of alcohol)

PT: No, sir. Thank you. (politely)

AT: A man what don't drink, best have his reasons, my lad. (With a crocked smile)

PT: Mean in' no disrespect, sir. (With an uncomfortable

expression)

PAGE 5 AT: bad luck to leave a toast unfinished my, lad. (With a sense of authority)

PT: I would -- I had understood it's 'giants' regulations, sir. (PT stops himself to rephrase, more respectfully. It's not easy for him to be well-mannered. He takes his time, so as not to get the old man angry)

PT (cont.): From theme's manual, sire. Aren't you trying for trouble? Sire.

AT: Did not picture you was a reading man. YOUNG--OLD Then you do as I say. That's in year book, too. (Angrily, with a sense of arrogance)

PT: yes, sire. (Bending his head down) (Throws the liquid down without the AT seeing and fills the cup with water at the sink) AT: The cistern needs a-looking in to. One of year duties, lad. Or didn't you read yourself about it? Polishing, swabbing. Swabbing and polishing. You will clean the brass and the clockwork, and you can tidy the quarters after. There is well-more to be mended outside. Ye be misbehaving again ye be facing consequences PT monologue the worker is a nice chap. He mostly kept to himself although we never talked, he was not much of a trouble he did his work and never misbehaved in the work. he was good at work too. This does not stop the wicked old from tormenting the poor soul. Day after day the boy looked paler and paler by the end of the week, I could not even look at him. He was nothing but bones and skin. I could not see him for the next week as he was supposed to work in the smelter room. All I could hear from the room above are howls of the old man to work fast. Oh, the poor chap I feel sorry for him. But I never confronted the old man as he holds my money. Night after night passed, I searched everywhere I turned the place upside down I could not even find a penny anywhere I wondered where could the old man put his all money. I looked in the oil barrels all the lockers all the cabins all the places.as I was looking I heard a slight noise from the stairs above I quickly adjusted the place and left from there hide under the stairs the old walked in I see his hands tremble he is probably drunk. The old seem desperate he clearly realized that someone entered his room. He ran to the PAGE 6 furnace room quickly I followed him quickly but silently under the heavy metal table lies heavy box probably a locker I hide behind the door and slowly observed him. He drew a bunch of keys from them a large key with a shape of snake carved on it. I could not believe my eyes the box illuminated a weird golden light from it must probably be gold or diamonds or something probably valuable. He swiftly locked it and rushed to the furnace I realized he must be looking for me and the young chap. I quickly jumped out of the window to get to the oil room. My ankle is sprained but I hide the pain little suspicion to the old devil he will cut my pay. He must have checked the chap upstairs. I heard stairs as steps approaching, I rushed to the oil can and started filling it. He looked with his vulture eyes. In a growly voice what happened to your ankle it looks like a fat disgusting wretch. One of the barrels fell on it sire. Mumbling to himself so that must be the sound I heard. He took a big bottle from the table below and starts drinking it and shouted at me to get back to work. Slowly he went upstairs I reassured myself with the sprained ankle he must have thought I could not climb the stairs. I could not shut my eye that night all I could think of are weird day dreams about the box and living with it in my own place in the woods far away from this cursed place. Slowly the dreams turned into an obsession whenever I got few moments to spare, I went to the place and looked at the box. The boy never minded me he just gets on with his work. Day after day I grew sick of the smell of oil and the disgusting sounds of metal works. All I could think of is the glorious light from the box all the wealth it contains. My hold on reality slowly started fading all the wild fancies struct me I could not even tell if I was awake or sleeping. The enchantment oh!!! The light. The old man became nervous too he barely left the quarters he never left the keys anywhere. They were always in his pockets whenever he approached me, I could hear there clinking noise. He grew more and more suspicious of the boy he changed his shifts from night to day and always looked from his quarters into the furnace hall he works. I clearly noticed the old started abusing the boy more and more as his suspicion grew. He reduced the boys supplies and made him even starve more. I was too much occupied with my own fantasies of the box to care about the boy. One day I tried to sneak into the old man's room to search for the keys as he was taking a bath in the room next to it. I snuck into the room like an owl about to hunt a rat I did not even made the faintest noise. Suddenly I heard footsteps approaching from the stairs I panicked and hit a lamp. Oh!! the devil it fell to the floor I quickly placed the lamb on the table and hid under the stair case I small amount of kerosene fell on to my shirt. The old man shouted who is there how dare you come into my quarters. The poor chap probably afraid of the old man started running up the stairs. The old man drew a big shot gun from the drawer above and loaded it and filled with gun powder and started chasing the boy. As the chase pursued, I slowly snuck out of there and looked out of the window from there. Both disappeared into the forest. I quickly went to the furnace and took the box and hid it under the table in my quarters. I went to the window and looked if the old man is returning. I heard a loud shot and few moments later a cry for help another faint sound I heard I knew he did it. Fear ensued on me I sweated like never before. I saw the old man coming out of the forest. I quickly covered the table under which I hid the box with all the sheets I could find. I went out as if I knew nothing had happened and asked him what was the loud sound from the forest. He looked at me and said its nothing probably the hunters must be hunting for wild boar. Enough, roaming outside get back to work I don't pay you for hearing noises in the woods. As he was leaving, I noticed that my shirt was covered in kerosene. I quickly turned around to see the old man trying to load his gun I quickly grabbed a stone from the PAGE 7 ground and swiftly by strongly smashed his head!!!! Just like that it was done he was no more I grabbed his keys and ran to the box. In a brief second of time, I looked at the window there was no old man he must be following me without delay I lifted the box and started running into the forest. I realized something was following me into the forest. I hid under a tree I saw the old man coming he was slowly approaching panting with blood all over him. I waited there for him to come close so that I could attack him. I swiftly delivered a blow to his back as he was falling, he shot the gun. I did not even notice what happened then I started running with the box. After a mile or 2 later I realized my shirt was covered in blood. My senses are slowly leaving me I started to faint. Narrator's voice all that was left are 3 dead bodies in an abandoned place and a rusty demonic place and cursed box filed with the mysterious light.

Meet the Co-Authors

Komal Joshi

She is a creative soul with a spark of magic and the desire of doing more leaving a little bit of glitter smile and laughter wherever she goes. Forever a new girl on the block who loves Bollywood and all things media and who is always ready to lend a hand and try her 100% with a smile. Komal is a Gujarati girl from the UK, but she is forevermore, a proud Indian from her heart.

Uma Bokil

Uma Bokil is a freelance writer and editor based in Pune. She has been writing since the age of four and loves to talk endlessly about books, stories, food, and life. She has co-authored multiple anthologies and looks forward to her solo novel someday.

Halo Golwin

Halo Golwin is not merely a symbol but an epithet for Golwin's whimsical friend, who inspired him to exercise personal freedom through writing. With the might of the pen, Halo Golwin's works often bring out the absurd in the mundane and utilise humour to amplify the insane. If you are an avid lover of poetry and art, do visit @not_a_blank_slate_anymore on Instagram!

Arya

In the realm of creative minds, there exists an aspiring Science Fiction and Fantasy writer who goes by the pen name Arya. With a fervent desire to forge a genre unlike any other, Arya finds solace in crafting imaginative worlds, breathing life into captivating characters, and propelling engrossing storylines. The art of storytelling has been ingrained in Arya's existence for as long as memory serves, fuelling a passion that knows no bounds.

being_me_av

Abhishek Agarwal aka AV is an XLRI Jamshedpur Alumni, a Serial Entrepreneur, Founder & CEO of LRA Unified Group, Bangalore which has a strong vision for making lives better with a social impact. AV brands himself as being_me_av and is also an Internationally Authenticated & Certified Business, Leadership, Life Coach and have coached, mentored thousands of Business Owners & Individuals Globally. He writes fiction, non-fiction contents on various topics and is a Thought Leader, Visionary, Polymath, Humanitarian. He shares deep love for Food, Nutrition, Running & Travelling and has a life motto: 'Don't Live A Life, Live A Lifestyle'! You can reach out to him @being_me_av across Social Media platforms.

Didriksha Chakraborty

A young poet in her teenage who believes her pen is enough to scream all the words that her heart wants to express but her voice fails to. Not only a poet, but she is also a blooming musician trying to pave her way in this world. She has already participated in many anthologies which you all can check out to read more of her work.

Deborshmi Nath

Deborshmi Nath is an 11-year-old or 6th grade Indian girl who currently lives in Zhuhai, a city in China, with her parents. She studies at QSI International School of Zhuhai where she finds friends and teachers around to support her. Along with her schooling, Deborshmi is also interested in Indian classical dance, Ballet, Swimming, Guitar, Wing Chun, and Singing. Her mother tongue is Bengali, but she is also able to speak English, Chinese, and Hindi; Spanish and French are two of the languages that she attends class at school but hasn't gotten very fluent yet.

Aanika Gajendragad

Aanika is a 15-year-old home schooler that left school to focus on her career as a writer. She has loved to write from the age of 9 and making a career out of it seemed like the best choice. Moreover, math and science never interested her. She has written about 30 short stories, few of which have been included in anthologies. She also writes blogs and articles.

Sandhita Agarwal

Sandhita is a software developer by profession but a hippie at heart. She likes to travel the world and meet different people. She completed her Masters in AI and ML from LJMU, UK. She is one of the authors showcased in the anthology Minds@Work2. When not writing or coding, she can be found listening to true crime documentaries and reading up on conspiracies. She lives with her spunky cocker spaniel in Bangalore and hopes to have a tête-à-tête with Salman Rushdie one day.

Valerie Hernandez

Valerie Hernandez is an economist by profession but a writer by love. Originally from Mexico, she currently works as a digital strategist but loves music, literature, traveling, and telling stories so much that she collaborates independently with various digital publications. Her first novel, “Frente al Escenario” will soon be published in English and as an audio experience. She also has an original collaboration on the UNTANGLED anthology.

HyderK

HyderK is your regular Sci-fi enjoyer from Hyderabad. He loves reading, writing, and watching movies and shows. Join him and embark on a space adventure filled with engaging action through an alien world on the brink of a galactic civil war.

Kai Jennings

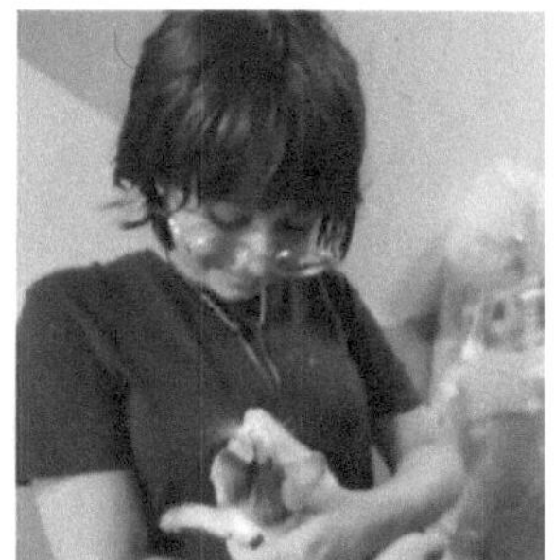

Kai Jennings is an Indian writer who was inspired by Rick Riordan. They are demi non binary and gender fluid and want to let people know they aren't alone.

Debjyoti Das

Debjyoti, an author, a poet, and professionally a teacher of English language and literature is from Kolkata, India. A prolific writer who received Humanitarian Award from a London based international NGO for inspiring humanity worldwide during pandemic lockdown with his poems in 2020. His solo book of love poems, only for you, My Love has been published recently and instantly earned positive reviews and responses from the readers and well-wishers particularly from the young generation. Debjyoti has co-authored more than forty anthologies till now and received many awards and recognition for his contribution in the field of Literature.

Ananya Purba Sengupta

Ananya is an IT engineer by profession and a creative thinker by heart. She loves reading, writing exploring creative stuff. She started writing from a noticeably early age and enjoys putting down her thoughts on paper.